THEN YOU SAW ME

CARRIE AARONS

Do you want your **FREE** Carrie Aarons eBook?

All you have to do is **sign up for my newsletter**, and you'll immediately receive your free book!

To all the women who keep quiet but carry a big stick, this book is for you.

1

I t's the fighting that wakes me.

"You didn't text me at all, Bevan!"

Callum is shouting from somewhere in the kitchen, which just so happens to be located right beneath my bedroom in the floor plan of our college house.

"I was in the fucking library, you moron! Why the hell would I have been out on a Tuesday night? I'm not you and your buddies!"

Bevan's voice floats up through the floor, and I wince at how angry my best friend sounds. She and her boyfriend, two of the other people who live in this house, fight often. But a knock-down-drag-out before we've all had our morning coffee? That's not typical. This will lead to another breakup for sure, which will suck for the other housemates who have to endure the petty awkwardness.

"Then why were you avoiding me all night?" Her boyfriend, who she and I have known since freshman year of high school, cries.

"Maybe because I was studying! Some of us actually do that."

Shit, Bev sounds tired and furious, and yes, I can tell that even through the hardwood of my bedroom floor.

"They're at it again." Amelie, the other third of our trio of best friends, comes into my room without knocking and flops down on my bed.

Taya, Amelie, and Bevan. Best friends. Sisters minus the blood, although we'd once tried this Wiccan ritual and it had ended in a strange and somber manner. Anyway, we all met in the third grade and have been inseparable ever since.

Growing up in our Upstate New York town had been picturesque, and there wasn't a math test, homecoming, or football game we haven't faced together. So, we all decided on the same college. Fast forward to sophomore year, where we are now living in an off-campus house with three guys and us.

One of them being Callum, Bevan's high school sweetheart and currently very pissed off boyfriend. The two of them are toxic as hell and love each other to the moon and back. Amelie and I are used to it, but it doesn't make it any less annoying being woken up on hump day to a prelude to makeup sex.

"God, do you think we'll have to hear them screwing again?" I throw a pillow over my ears, but it doesn't dull the roar from the kitchen.

Am shrugs where she lies a few inches from me. "I'm not sure what's worse, the fighting or the fucking. Should we take a poll of the street? Because I swear, everyone outside these windows can hear them, too."

Prospect Street is the most desired road to live on if you're a college student at Talcott University, and we just happened to snatch up one of the best houses. It has six bedrooms, a kitchen that was updated after two thousand seventeen, three bathrooms so the girls don't have to share the one the two the boys decimate on a regular basis, and a basement fully worthy of parties. Six Prospect Street, our not so humble abode, also has the best backyard on the street since the owner put in a hot tub and is located closest to the bars we'll frequent when we turn twenty-one. Or when we can get decent fake IDs, whichever comes first.

There's no doubt, it's chaotic living with five other people, but I wouldn't change it for the world. We're a family, even if it's a dysfunctional one, and my college years, all one and a half of them, thus far, have been incredible because of it.

"Did you see Gannon off last night? Sorry, I was so tired." I stroke Am's white-blond hair as she lies in my lap.

"Yeah." Just one word and I can tell she's heartbroken to the depths of her soul.

Amelie may be my and Bevan's best friend, but she has a fourth in her book. A person who might be even slightly closer to her heart than the two of us, considering she's head over heels in love with him. Not that Gannon, our third male housemate, has a clue.

Case in point? He's just been chosen to compete on a reality TV dating show for college students, and he couldn't pack for Los Angeles fast enough. Amelie, the giving, caring, petite, curvy one of the three of us, is devastated. I don't know how long it will take for her to recover, but I hope this is the kick in the ass she needs.

I would never be mean about it, but I've seen Am pine for Gannon for *years*. And all he's done is brought other women around her and treated her like a kid sister. It's heartbreaking to watch, and I want my friend to be happy. I want her to fall in love with someone who truly appreciates her.

"Well, good. You and I can go out and celebrate our single life tonight. And revel in the fact that we're both not down there, screaming at someone we claim to love." I giggle, and Amelie high fives me.

We might be making fun of Bevan, but it's all in good fun.

The three of us don't hide barbs, jokes, or opinions from the others. Ours is the purest of friendships; we give the bad just as great as we take the good.

A lot of people probably judge the three of us for attending the same college. They accuse us of not growing, of not branching out to make new friends or experience the world. I know this because people have literally come up to me on the street in our hometown and sarcastically joked about the three of us being inseparable, to a fault.

It doesn't bother me much.

My two best friends and I have our reasons, and we don't need to explain them. Maybe the biggest underlying one is that we just love each other too much and don't want to be apart. Is that such a crime? There is no such thing that says you can't move out of your comfort zone, try new things and grow while doing it beside people you love.

There's Amelie, the nurturing sprite who wants to be a children's librarian, and that should tell you everything you need to know about her. Then Bevan, the spitfire who's as athletic as she is whip-smart. Bevan is an overachiever who is also good at every single thing she picks up. Well, I guess, except for her relationship.

And finally, me. The middle man, the glue. The laid-back one who could also throw insults if anyone did my friends wrong. I'm bendable; I fit between their strong wills and saccharine-sweet kindness. Where Amelie is the fairy princess and Bevan is all attitude in black, I'm the preppy, average-American kind of girl. My eyes are big and hazel, my hair a shade past chestnut, and while I keep myself in shape, I don't have the luscious curves or enviable muscles of my two friends.

I'm fine with all of that. I'm more than happy on a good day.

Well, except when I'm woken up by a screaming couple.

"We better go break that up," I grumble, rising out of bed.

Besides Callum and Gannon, who departed the house last night, our other male roommate is Scott. Who, honestly, is probably out sleeping in someone else's bed. Aside from Scott, the other five of us went to high school together. And while I like Scott as a friend, he makes horrible decisions in his dating life. Mostly, he just sleeps with way too many people and it gets him into sticky situations. Last year, a girl egged our house and dumped baby powder all over his car through the sun roof when he kissed her friend at a party.

Amelie and I make our way downstairs, sans bras or brushing our teeth, because who cares if Callum and Scott see us like this. Not only are they not interested, but no way in hell am I walking around my own house in a bra twenty-four seven.

"Ding ding, time to take a timeout." I take Bevan by the shoulders, and she tries to shrug me off.

"He's being a fucking dick!" she cries, looking to Am and me.

"Oh, come on, baby!" Callum starts to walk toward her, and Am steps in.

"Let's all cool down, okay? I'll make some breakfast, Bev, you go up and I'll bring you coffee—"

Just as Amelie is about to keep detailing her plan of attack in that calm, soothing way of hers, our doorbell rings.

"Huh?" I swing my head to it, just feet away. "Anyone expecting someone at the crack of dawn on Wednesday?"

Really, it's eight thirty, which to college students is pretty much the crack of dawn.

The doorbell rings again because we're all standing here, either staring at it or at Bevan and Callum, who are angrily staring at each other.

"Is someone going to get that?" Bevan harrumphs.

Callum, probably trying to get on her good side, walks to the door and opens it.

"Oh, shit, I forgot you were coming this morning, man. Come on in!"

My roommate then steps back to reveal the one person I would be mortified not to have a bra on in front of. Or the pimple cream still crusted on my chin. Don't get me started on how humiliated I am that I'm not done up to my fullest potential when the only guy I've ever wanted to notice me, and hasn't, just walked into my house.

There he is, standing in the middle of our crappy college house foyer with a black duffel plopped down beside him and a Talcott University hat pulled low on his forehead.

Sandy blond whiskers paint his sharp cheeks and dust along that jaw I've dreamed about for years. The botanical tattoo, comprised of ivy and other plants, snakes up from his right wrist and disappears under the T-shirt stretched over his bicep. I have to crane my neck to look at his beautifully rugged face, and I'm not a short woman.

Everything inside my belly clenches when those dark brown eyes, the color of creamy hot chocolate, roam over me and stop. He's the college version of Aleksander Skarsgård, and internally I'm freaking out that the sexy guy from that vampire show just invited himself in, even if I didn't allow him to enter the doorway.

"Meet our new roommate!" Callum announces the tall Norse god's presence, and I want to smack my best friend's boyfriend.

Had I known this was the person he'd gotten to sublet Gannon's room, I would have nixed it on the spot. There is absolutely no fucking way I can live with this guy. Hell has to be freezing over.

Austin Van Hewitt, the guy I've had a crush on since I could ascertain what a crush *was*, is moving in.

2

Six Prospect Street isn't a bad place to land on your feet.

It's close to the bars, I have my own room in the finished attic of the house, I'll be close to all the house parties going on away from campus, and hopefully, I won't have to answer to anyone. I don't know these people, so my last semester of senior year could be spent without having to explain myself or work out interpersonal conflicts.

When my roommate decided to move his girlfriend into our two-bedroom on-campus condo, it got a little crowded for me. We were friends, but not the tightest of buddies I have here, and I wasn't about to third wheel their honeymoon stage in my own house.

So when Callum, a kid I knew from back home, told me there was going to be a vacant room for the spring semester in their house, I jumped on the chance. Er, well, maybe I cautiously stepped into it.

Because now I'll be living with a bunch of people who know exactly who I am.

The perks of the house almost outweigh the fact that I'm living with a bunch of kids from my hometown. Not that I know them all that well, but I generally try to avoid anyone who knew me in high school.

Shit, not because I was an asshole or a bully. I feel like I'm probably explaining it all wrong, so let me introduce you to the Van Hewitt effect.

My family, for all intents and purposes, owns the town I grew up in. They paid for half the high school to be built when it was first constructed. My relatives own the liquor store; the library is named after our family; we throw the homecoming parade each year. At the summer carnival, my dad gives a speech, and my uncle is actually the mayor. My grandparent's farm is a hometown staple, and the locals shop there for meat and milk rather than the grocery store.

So, being a Van Hewitt comes with strings. Everyone knows who you are. I went to high school with six of my cousins. Our family is so big that Thanksgiving has to be held in a tent in my grandparent's backyard. And when someone in our hometown learns my last name, they want something from me. Guys want an in with my family for some weird reason; girls want to date me just to say they might get the Van Hewitt last name.

When I was ready to start picking colleges, it was pre-determined that I would go to Talcott. Almost every Van Hewitt had, and I'm not the type to buck against the family legacy. It only creates more drama, and Talcott is a good school. True, it's only forty minutes from my hometown of Webton, but I don't go home much.

I do, however, control who I hang out with here. And the fewer Webton kids I interact with, the better. I've created a social circle here who have no clue what my last name means or what pressures I carry because of it. I suppose that will change now, not that I owe much to my five roommates who I will only share a house with for four months.

Graduation is on the horizon, and I suppose a return to

Webton is in the cards. There are no careers in my chosen field of sports radio, but my dad wouldn't hear it. I'll go home, try to get a job at the crappy local station and make ends meet, or I'll end up working for one of the family businesses.

I rub my temples as all the frustrations I've been dealing with invade my mind. Senior year is supposed to be fun, the last taste of freedom. Instead, I find myself moving in the first week of the semester into a house with a bunch of kids who know exactly what family I come from, no less. Then there are the worries about getting a job and secretly applying to the kind of ones I want all over the country.

Heading down the three flights of stairs to the kitchen, I don't bump into a single soul. The house is quiet, and I assume some of my new housemates either have class or went to the fitness center before it's too busy. I need to get my ass over there, but lugging all my shit to the attic will probably suffice for today. Not that I'm complaining, having a whole floor to myself will be nice, even if it's a hike to get there.

As I get the lay of the land in the kitchen, a big open-air room with a huge island constructed of wood with a cutting board surface instead of granite or marble, I realize this might be the best decision I've made. My friends, the ones I should have taken up on their offer to live together last year when I had the chance, will love this place.

I'll have to convince my roommates to throw a party.

My water bottle is half full when I hear a noise in the hall, and I poke my head around the fridge to see who it is.

The brunette of the three girls living here is practically tiptoeing through the hallway like she doesn't want anyone to hear her. I smirk because she looks damn cute doing it, and because her ass is …

Incredible.

All the people living in this house, aside from Scott, who I was introduced to just ten minutes ago and didn't go to high school with, are two years behind me in our hometown. They were sophomores when I was a senior at Webton, as they are now at Talcott. So I don't quite remember any of them, aside from Callum, because we played sports together growing up.

It's a damn shame I don't remember her or didn't know her in high school because she's gorgeous. Long wavy brown hair, the color of autumn leaves, that she's taken down from the ponytail it looks like she slept in when I first entered the house. The prettiest hazel eyes you've ever seen. They verge on the edge of blue, but the green and brown swirl together in there too, like a Monet painting where all the colors melt into each other. I got such a good look at them because she was practically scowling at me when I first walked in to meet everyone.

My eyes? They could barely keep to themselves. Her nipples had been poking through that threadbare T-shirt, and those long legs were on full display under the baggy pair of boxers floating dangerously low on her narrow hips. I wonder idly, now, if those belong to a guy. Be a shame if they did.

Getting involved with a roommate is probably the worst thing I could do, especially a girl who's from Webton and knows exactly where to find me when I leave here.

But if she came into my room, drunk, after a party? Hell, no, I wouldn't be turning her down.

Just as I begin to daydream what it might be like for her to climb into my lap, to hold her hips and rock her against the shameless appendage in my pants that is currently stiffening, she turns.

And looks like a goddamn deer in headlights.

My mouth spreads wide in a smile, and I'm about to open it to start a conversation when she quickly walks out the front door. In a gaggle of noise, the other two females who live here follow, and Callum's girlfriend slams the door shut.

This is going to be an interesting semester: new house, co-ed roommates, my entire future on the line. My mind wanders as I cap my water and go upstairs to unpack.

Taya. *Taya*, I think that's her name.

Yeah, living here won't be so bad if I get to see Taya walk around in the outfit she'd come down in this morning.

"I'm going to murder your boyfriend."

My mood is a toss-up between sour and stressed to the max as we walk into the Sunrise Diner.

"You'll have to get in line, because he's currently on my shit list, as well," Bevan grumbles, tossing a lock of midnight-black hair over her shoulder.

The Sunrise is packed, per usual, since it's one of the only places to eat near campus. Talcott University sits atop a hill, and our street is about a five-minute drive up it. While there are a ton of restaurants and shops down on Commons Avenue near our house, the Sunrise is the only place to eat a quick bite before driving to class. Since we don't have meal plans on campus anymore, we usually stop here a couple mornings out of the week.

And today, I was definitely in need of a pancake fix.

Amelie puts our names in as I wave to two girls sitting in a booth that I know from an International Studies course I took last year.

Shortly thereafter, we're escorted to our table, a four-top right by the window overlooking the lake view Talcott University is known for. Nestled in the Finger Lakes of Upstate New York, my chosen college is as beautiful as it is frigid in the winters. Cayuga Lake is its crown jewel, a massive body of water where the college students swim, water-ski, and congregate in the two or three warm months that exist up here. The whole college town is built on the hill that slopes above the lake, and the neighborhoods are winding one-way streets all funneling into Commons Avenue, the trendy downtown area that turns into Drunk Central past the hour of eleven p.m. The three biggest bars in a fifty-mile radius exist there, and I've only managed to sneak in underage once. Not that we didn't try. A lot.

"Three chocolate milks?" Randi, our usual waitress, smiles as she walks up to our table.

"And a coffee, please. It's been a morning." Bevan gives her a pained look.

"Thanks, Rand." Amelie is her usual cheerful self, but I can see the bags under her eyes.

She's probably been crying in her room since she dropped Gannon off at the airport. Imagine driving the man you love to a flight he's taking to go fall in love with someone else. Even in the midst of my internal freak-out, my heart ached for her.

Randi brought back our chocolate milks and Bevan's coffee, took our orders, and then we sipped. Chocolate milk is a call to our childhood days, and we can't quit them, no matter how mature lattes or cold brews would have seemed.

"So, are we going to talk about the A-bomb that Callum dropped?" Amelie focuses on me.

I saw only one more glimpse of Austin as the three of us girls left for breakfast. He was in the kitchen, filling his water bottle at the sink. I tried to tiptoe out, but he must have bat ears because he turned and smiled, and my stomach dropped to my feet.

At least I had on mascara, a bit of blush, and my hair had been curled by that point. However, the image of my rumpled, sleep-worn face and body were probably seared into his mind. Jesus, I'll have to start wearing a bra and lipstick around the house now, won't I?

"*Que diable vais-je faire? Je ne peux pas vivre avec lui!*" I mutter into my palms and then press them to my eyes.

"Uh-oh, she's gone full Lindsay Lohan in *The Parent Trap*. We need those pancakes, stat!" Bevan looks at me like I'm crazy.

As a foreign languages major, I tend to switch to my best second language when I'm really upset. Which is French. I also speak fluent Spanish, Italian, and plan to master Arabic and Mandarin before I graduate.

I want to work for a government agency, specifically the United Nations, if I can swing it. My nerves are too jumpy for the FBI and CIA, plus they dig into your life. A lot. I don't have much to hide, but I've definitely smoked too much pot or something else trivial that would exclude me. There is something about going to work for an agency that promotes peace and unity, though I know it may be unrealistic at best, that speaks to me.

"Sorry. I'm just wondering how the hell I'm ever going to live with Austin freaking Van Hewitt?" I do a dramatic sob and flop my arms and chin onto the table. "He saw me in my freaking pajamas, not even matching ones, with pimple cream on my face."

"If it makes you feel any better, he didn't notice you for the entirety of our lives in Webton, so he probably didn't even notice." Bevan does her best sympathetic pat on my arm.

Yeah, remember when I told you we're brutally loving and brutally honest? Bevan is the most honest one of us all. She has serious intimacy issues from her dad disappearing and showing up out of the blue every other year until high school graduation, which is probably why her relationship with Callum is such a mess.

"Gee, thanks. Makes me feel so much better." I roll my eyes at her.

Am shrugs. "She kind of has a point. I mean, how long did you crush on him? Or are we still crushing on him? I thought that ended when he blew you off at that homecoming dance—"

"Please, do we have to spend this breakfast recounting the most embarrassing moments of my life?" The annoyed growl that works its way out of my throat is accompanied by a hunger pang.

Where are my goddamn pancakes?

"I just want to make sure you're okay with this. It can still be remedied if you're not. Callum should have given us a heads-up." Amelie's fingers lace with mine across the table.

"Yeah, that dickhead. He gets on me for studying too late but forgets to inform the entire house that he found someone to sublet the attic bedroom and it just so happens to be Austin Van Hewitt?" Bevan seethes in her seat next to Am.

Amelie gives her a warning look. "We'll get to your problems in a second, but you know I'm going to tell you the same thing I always have."

The two of us have been telling Bevan for months now that she and Callum should break up. For at least a month or two, and he should move out. Yes, I love Callum like a brother. Yes, it would make the housing situation messy. But the two of them are toxic. They couldn't have a healthy relationship, and it's slowly eroding both of their souls. You can practically see it.

"Fine. Taya first. She's the more pressing issue," Bev agrees and turns to me with an expectant expression.

I hate the way they both study me, Amelie's blush-pink blouse perfectly laying across her enviable chest and Bevan's leather moto jacket intimidating. My best friends are a seriously scary package, and I throw up my hands.

"I don't know what you want me to say! I'm not the one who did this."

Randi returns with our food, thank God, and I get a reprieve for a few minutes as we all shovel pancakes and bacon into our mouths. I didn't go out last night, but this week's set of quizzes was annoying and exhausting. Why does every college professor insist on testing your knowledge during week two of a new semester?

Amelie breaks the silence. "Tay, we know you didn't do this. But you've had a crush on the guy for like ten years. And he doesn't know it. And now he's living in our house."

I roll my eyes. "Give me more credit than that. I've barely seen him in the last four years, you don't think I've moved past it?"

"The way you stared at him like an alien had just invaded Prospect Street would say you have not. Maury determines that is a lie," Bevan cracks, and I scowl at her.

"Fine. I mean, seeing him brought back some memories. Some feelings. But like you said, he's never known I existed. It shouldn't change now. What does it matter if he's living in the house?"

I'm trying to act nonchalant, and my best friends see right through my bullshit.

The truth is, it matters. *A lot.*

I've been half in love with Austin Van Hewitt since ... well, probably the fifth grade. The first time I ever saw him was at a town carnival, and he and his seventh grade friends were goofing around on the Ferris wheel. They kept getting out of their cars and hanging from the bars, and the ride attendant was so pissed. But in typical pre-teen boy fashion, they were obnoxious and cocky enough to stick around and laugh about it.

Everyone thought they were effortlessly cool. Especially me, but only about one boy in particular. Austin. With his young

Justin Bieber haircut, smile that made my heart skip a beat, and wrist full of woven bracelets made by some seventh grade girls ... he was my heartthrob.

Then I learned who his family was, they practically own my hometown, and it was even harder not to be obsessed with him. And obsessed is the right word. I daydreamed about him all hours of the day, as one does about the boy they think they're going to marry even though they've never talked to him or been in the same room as him.

As I got older, the stupid little crush became a living, breathing thing. When I got to high school, things intensified. I got pretty, or as pretty as I'd ever be. I watched him in the halls at our shared lunch period. I was on the freshman girls' basketball team, while he played varsity for the boys, and I'd moon over him at practices. I thought someday he would notice me.

Cue my sophomore homecoming, where my mission was to get him to talk to me finally. Or at least dance with me. And dance we did. I'd been scooting myself over to his position all night, trying to look cool and not desperate. But my plan was for him to notice me. Notice the effortlessly beautiful high school sophomore with hair that was too stick straight since I had wrestled my waves with a hair tool and eyeliner out the wazoo.

Austin bit. He finally noticed me, and as the opening chords of "*Yellow*" by Coldplay floated over the dance floor, he took me in his arms. We swayed; he said something about how he liked my sparkly navy dress. They were the best four minutes of my life.

And then the song ended, a rap beat came on, he grabbed a different girl, and I was forgotten. For the entirety of that year, until he graduated and went off to Talcott two years before I arrived, he never once noticed me again. I was devastated. I'm pretty sure I took a sick day when I realized he never even asked my name.

My crush on him is—*was*—completely irrational. I know most everything I've learned about Austin Van Hewitt through hallway gossip, secondhand conversations, and that one dance we had. As ridiculous as my feelings were, I just couldn't turn them off.

Coming to Talcott and knowing he attended college here as well gave me a spark of hope. But we've barely run into each other. And my crush has cooled off. It's been over four years since I drooled over him, since I cried when he didn't fall madly in love with me after one dance.

I'm more mature now; I have things I'm focusing on and a list of requirements that I want in a boyfriend. It's why I don't date much; I'm too picky. Who even knows if Austin actually fits my perfect mold.

With a defiant nod that my friends look bewildered over, I settle it within my own soul.

This will not affect me. Who cares if Austin is living under the same roof that I am? I can be an adult, I'm not in love with him anymore, and we barely know each other. I'm a strong, independent, valuable woman who doesn't need a man to make her whole.

Absolutely nothing is going to happen between us, and I am completely okay with that.

Now, if only I can convince my rapidly panicking heart.

4

Two days after I move in, we have our first house meeting.

I've barely seen any of my housemates in that forty-eight-hour period, what with our overlapping class schedules, gym time, some of them having jobs, and just generally missing each other. Scott seems like the party kid, already staying out both nights I've lived here, and the girls definitely like their beauty sleep.

I've already been witness to the sounds of Callum and Bevan loudly fucking, Amelie's pretty singing voice, and the hot water going out since I'd been the last to hop in the shower.

The only person I've really not seen at all is Taya, but now I am sitting right across from her. All of those shining mahogany waves are flowing over her shoulders, her lips are painted a shade of deep mauve, and thin gold hoops hang from her ears. The tank she has on barely grazes the top of her belly button, and with the way she's wearing those black jeans, I could make out every curve of her hips, ass, and waist.

Damn, but she's making it hard to focus. It's a good thing I haven't run into her much, or I'd be in trouble.

It's six p.m. on Friday, and Scott, the only non-Webton room-mate, picked up pizzas for dinner while we have this meeting. I grabbed a few cases of beer, since I'm the only one over twenty-one, and we're all seated around the large wooden coffee table in the living room. The room is more suitable as a dance floor at a party, it's that big, and I'm sure it's been turned into one many times over the years by the many people who have lived in this house.

I can't wait to see how crazy this place gets tonight. Not only is this our first house meeting, but I've convinced my housemates to throw a party. Not that they needed much convincing, they said they basically held one at least once every weekend because so many of their underage friends couldn't get into the bars. If they got turned away, they came here because it was close, and eventually, the party just kind of happened.

"Okay, rule number one: if there is a tissue box on the door, do not enter that room. Freaky things are happening in there." Callum points at me.

"Really? That's rule number one about respectfully living in this house?" Bevan rolls her eyes at her boyfriend, then picks up a slice of pepperoni and takes a big bite.

"Why a tissue box? Isn't it a sock? Or a girl's hair tie?" I question, taking a sip of my beer.

Amelie, who is sitting above us all on the couch while munching on a Caesar salad, laughs. "Well, we did that at first. But Scott is an almost-sleepwalker and kept being able to twist the handles with those things. We improvised and started using empty tissue boxes. He can't get in, and everyone can be on their merry, orgasmic way."

Scott nearly spits his beer out as he jokes, "Good one, Ams."

She smiles and nods her head at her comedic timing.

"The most important rule in this house is: don't eat anyone

else's shit. Label your own shit. If I catch you eating my food, I'll end you." Bevan slices her finger across her throat.

I hold my hands up in surrender because this girl fucking scares me. "No complaints from me about either of those rules. I'll have my own mini-fridge upstairs, so you won't have to worry about me taking space. On the other front, I'll remember to grab an empty tissue box."

My eyes flit over to Taya as I say that, and she's looking anywhere but at me. I wonder how many times I'll catch a tissue box on her door. The thought both intrigues me and makes me a little jealous. The girl is gorgeous, and I wonder at the same time if I could be the guy to put a tissue box on her doorknob.

I'm pretty sure I've been staring at her for too long because she's chewing her lip, and Amelie is looking at me curiously. I turn back to the group and hide my distracted mind by scarfing down my pizza.

"Always park behind the person you know will be leaving the house last the next day. You'll get to know the shuffle of cars pretty quick. But since we have three spots, double stacked, it gets annoying if you're blocked in and have to leave first."

This rule comes from Scott, who seems chill. I didn't realize we already knew each other from playing intramural basketball, and he's a baller on the court.

"Got it. And if I do, just yell at me, and I'll move my car." I look around the circle.

"Besides that, I think we're golden. I mean, normal human rules apply. Do your laundry, don't be stanky, if you want to smoke, go outside ..." Callum looks off like he's trying to come up with other things that are common decency.

"Don't worry. You guys will barely notice I'm around," I assure them.

"Says the prom king." Bevan sneers at me, then smiles sweetly.

I choke on my beer. "Touché. But if it makes a difference, I would have given away that crown so fast, it wasn't even funny."

These people, who were two years younger than I was in high school, probably think I relished that Mr. Popular title. They'd be surprised if they knew just how wrong they were.

The way I talk about my prom crown has Taya cocking her head to the side to examine me. I don't love that she's trying to peel back the layers, to study my vulnerabilities, but I do love that she's looking at me.

I've never loved eyes on me because it's been that way my entire life—expectations, attention, responsibility. I wish it would go away, and Talcott has given me that reprieve somewhat, but now I'm right back in the lion's den.

But when she looks at me ... I don't know. It doesn't feel like she wants any of those things. I don't feel on edge or like she's about to ask me about the Van Hewitt family tree. It's strange for someone who I've only spent a little bit of time with to put me at such ease.

My bullshit radar, my judgment meter, is pretty spot on. It has to be when I've been used so many times in my life.

So it's curious that no alarms are going off when I think about this girl. Taya North is about to become a very interesting roommate.

I just wonder if she has any rules of her own she'll demand I follow.

Cardi B and Megan Thee Stallion's "*WAP*" booms through the house, and bodies grind together everywhere.

My head bobs in time to the raunchy, catchy song, and I can just imagine taking a girl up to the third floor and thrusting into her in time to the beat.

Yeah, I'm fucking horny. It's been a month since I've gotten laid, since I had all of my roommate turmoil from day one of the semester. Before that, I was home, and it's easier to keep my dick in my pants than have word getting around town about who I'm sleeping with.

But tonight? I'm a half-cocked shotgun ready to unleash. The point of this party isn't to find a fuck buddy, but it'll be the best side effect.

I don't mean to sound so callous, but sometimes a guy just needs sex, right? A lot of the girls I've encountered in my three and a half years at college want the same exact thing. No strings, a space to experiment, and a good time that leads to mutual pleasure. I'm all for that, especially if it means there are no expectations that I'll be a boyfriend to anyone. Not only do I not have time for a relationship with all that I want to accomplish, but my love life is just one more thing my family could potentially control. No thanks.

"Vanny!"

I hear my nickname bellowed across the room and turn to see my best friend at Talcott, Brian, lumber over to me. Brian is a linebacker on the football team and weighs about double my body weight. He's the nicest guy you'll ever meet and an engineering whiz. Talcott's football team is division three, so he's really only playing for fun and some scholarship money. When he graduates, he'll be working at some top-tier firm in New York City, or at least that's his plan.

Secretly, I wish I could go too. We'd be roommates, and I've told him once or twice I'd consider it. Working and living in the Big Apple? Among some of the most famous radio stations in the country? Talk about my fucking dream.

I push it out of my head as he slaps me on the back. "Glad you could make it. Are Gio and Evan here?"

My other two closest friends at Talcott must be around here somewhere. They would have told me they weren't coming. Gio and I are both broadcast radio majors, while Evan met us at an intramural flag football game sophomore year and the three of us clicked. Brian and I were roommates freshman year by coincidence and the housing process, and the four of us just made a unit. We watch out for each other here and have had some fun-ass times. I'm going to miss them after graduation.

Brian nods. "They're running the pong table in the basement. Sick new house, by the way. Totally worth going through all that shit. Except you always should have lived with us."

"I know." I shake my head and sigh. "You know the shit with my dad ..."

My dad didn't think it was the right thing to do for a Van Hewitt to live off campus. Why? I have no fucking clue. But if I didn't live in an on-campus apartment or dorm, he wasn't paying for my senior year. That's seriously what he said. When the situation got so bad that I told my parents I had to move, he told me that I'd be paying my room and board out of my trust fund. It wasn't much of a threat, since I wouldn't feel any tightness in my own pockets, but it was more the meaning of it.

What kind of parent doesn't want their child to be happy? If it meant leaving a crappy situation, that was only crappy in the first place because of said parent's irrational rule, and moving to one that made that child content ... wasn't that a good thing? I don't know why I keep expecting my parents to be any different. They've only shown me moderate disappointment and annoyed judgment my entire life.

"Yeah, what a prick. But at least you got a sick house now! And close to the bars. You know I'm going to be crashing here once in a while when I can't make it back up the hill." Brian booms out a laugh.

"I've got the attic to myself, so you're always invited." I chuckle, sipping the rum and Coke Callum mixed in a Solo cup for me just before the party really started.

"Let's do a shot, we have to celebrate!" Brian wields a bottle of tequila from the kitchen counter and finds two shot glasses.

I'm not going to disagree.

I'm normally a little more controlled with my drinking, sticking to beer or going low-key with a glass of whiskey hanging with friends. Once you're over twenty-one, getting blackout drunk isn't as exciting as it is when you're legally not allowed to do so.

Tonight, though? I'm celebrating. Someone offers me a shot? I'm in. Beer pong? Flip cup? Funnel? I'm your guy.

There is just something lighter about moving into this house, getting out of my weird other living situation, and falling in with a new crowd.

Then, of course, there is my very interesting new roommate.

Taya. *Christ.* When she walked down those stairs tonight, my tongue nearly fell out of my head. She'd changed out of her little tank and jeans ensemble into a skintight, fire engine red dress. All of those mahogany curls were flowing down her back, and her olive-skinned shoulder blades peeked out from under them. I've never found shoulder blades attractive, but hers gave me a semi.

I can't stop following her with my eyes, tracking her like prey in my line of sight. Something primal is happening, and I know she feels it too. While setting up for the party, I found myself completing tasks anywhere around her, finding any reason to stand near her or talk to her.

After two shots with Brian, I wander off to find my other friends—or maybe in search of the girl who won't leave my thoughts.

My body buzzes with alcohol, happy and goofy. I'm the friendliest drunk you'll ever meet, and I smile at almost everyone I pass. The layout of the house is pretty easy to navigate. There are four bedrooms on the second floor, my attic bedroom on the third, and then the first floor is comprised of the cathedral-ceilinged living room, open-concept kitchen, and a dining room that is mostly used to store empty beer boxes or serve as a study space. All of the furniture in each room has either been covered with tarps, to prevent spills, or pushed to the side so that the aging light brown hardwood can be used as a dance floor.

I was amazed as they set up for the party, but I shouldn't have been. It's not just rowdy guys who live here; my female roommates have a system so that we can party until the wee hours, but also keep our couch stain-free and comfortable to watch movies on the next day.

I find myself at the basement stairs, the noise from the lower level bubbling up at me. The basement is like any other; a bare-bones college party space with gray cinderblock walls and gray concrete floors. The girls strung fairy lights all over the walls, giving it some ambiance, and there were two huge folding tables in the center. One is being used for beer pong, and the other for flip cup. At the back of the basement is a bar, some old piece of crap Callum's dad donated to the house when they all moved in.

And across the room, I find who I'm looking for—a beautiful girl in a knockout red dress.

"Hi." I smile at her as I walk right over, the alcohol buzzing through my veins.

"Hi." Taya leans against one of the support poles in the basement, smirking into her red cup.

"How is your night?" Leaning in allows me a whiff of her perfume, something flowery with a hint of cupcake.

I have to hold in a snort, because I just thought the word *cupcake* in my head, and that is definitely not smooth.

"Pretty good. Though I lost at beer pong." She pouts, and I want to catch that plump lower lip between my teeth.

"It's because you had the wrong partner." My dick jumps in my pants as I say it.

Her hazel eyes flash, unmistakable desire in them. "I guess you'll have to come find me earlier, next time."

"Well, I'm here now. How about we go upstairs and ... dance?" I grin, shameless in my approach.

What I really want to do is take her upstairs to my room, but I don't want to come on too strong. I do, however, think it's not too forward to take her to the dance floor and use it as an excuse to put my hands all over her.

"Oh, Austin. Austin, Austin, *Austin*. The guy who flirted with all the pretty girls in high school."

Something like suspicion and caution shoots down my spine, killing a little bit of my buzz. I almost forgot, for a moment, that Taya went to my high school. That she's known who I am for years, that she is fully aware of who my family is.

That age-old mistrust sneaks up on me, stealing all the flirty energy I've been sending her way. Why did she have to say that?

"Did I?" I eye her, and she's not aware that she just spoiled some of my fun.

Taya's head bobs on a nod, and even though I'm bordering on the edge of annoyed, I can't help but be attracted to her. She's a little goofy, which is endearing with how pretty she is. Some girls are beautiful and intimidating, and it makes them seem untouchable. But Taya is gorgeous and barely acknowledges it. Whenever we've been around each other, she's joking or laughing, which only adds to her appeal and charm.

"You were Mr. Popular, duh. All the girls wanted a chance with Austin Van Hewitt." She snorts into her cup as she takes a drink.

She's drunk. I know that. So am I. But her words have officially turned me off. I hate being handled like I'm some prize to win, and this interaction is no longer what I sought her out for.

If we hooked up, would she run back to all her Webton friends to brag about it? Would she hold some misguided notion that she was marrying into the Van Hewitt family? It's happened before, as crazy as it sounds.

And as much as I am into Taya and some no-strings-attached fun, I don't want the things that *would* come attached.

"Hey, I'll catch you later, okay?" I rub her arm in a friendly gesture, pissed that my fingertips spark when they touch her skin.

I almost break, because goddamn, she feels like velvet, but hold strong knowing that this is probably a mistake all the way around. A girl from my hometown, my roommate, a sophomore who has two more years left at Talcott.

"Oh." Taya frowns, her hazel eyes turning down. "Okay."

Fuck. I don't want to walk away, especially seeing how disappointed she is. But her words ring in my head, and I can't get over that mental block.

I flash her a smile and wave with the hand not holding my rum and Coke, then turn and walk away.

My drink is finished before I hit the basement stairs, and I'm off in search of some more alcohol to numb this feeling.

He flirted with me. Of his own accord, with a hundred other girls around.

I lie in my bed, hugging one of the eight pillows I always sleep with to my chest like some lovesick teen. I mean, I guess I kind of am, even though I am already twenty.

Austin Van Hewitt had sought me out at the party, talked me up, and I was quite sure something would have happened. Maybe he wasn't going to try anything with how many drinks I'd had.

I admit, I was drunk. Okay, I was past drunk. I wasn't blackout to the point where I didn't remember anything, but I was definitely a little brown out. There were pieces of the night that were fuzzy, because I'd been so nervously chugging on my cup all night before he found me that I was wasted.

There is a vague memory of Austin walking away instead of taking me to dance ... I think he asked me to dance? I was a little miffed that I wasn't in his bed, or at least able to remember a kiss. We definitely didn't have one of those, though I'd been hoping it would happen last night.

God, how pathetic am I? I talked a big game to Amelie and

Bevan at the diner about how I'm not affected by him. That my crush was long gone and we could exist as roommates.

Then our first big party happened and all the fairy tale Cinderella dreams had come true. I thought the prince would finally come and notice me, and he had, but at midnight I'd turned back into the pumpkin.

Would it happen again? Looking up at the ceiling as if willing it to open up and reveal Austin so I could ask him, I wiggle my toes. The giddy energy rolling off of me is ridiculous, but I can't believe he actually noticed me. I need to get a grip because if it doesn't happen again and I have to keep living in this house with him, I know I'll be heartbroken.

Sheesh, I really am pathetic. Plus, I don't have a lot of hot little numbers like the one I wore last night. I brought my A-plus game, and I'm not in his bed.

Okay, so the fire-engine red dress that looked like a second skin might have been a bit obvious, but it worked. I could feel Austin's eyes on me as we set up for the party. And for the first time since I started crushing on him, I felt powerful in this dynamic.

And for once in my life, I wanted all the attention on me.

I'm good at fading into the background, blending in, and being the one that doesn't upset the balance. I play my part, even though it isn't front and center or superstar of the team. I've been doing it since birth.

My cell vibrates on the bed next to me, and it's as if my mother's ears are ringing.

Don't get me wrong. I love my family. I love my parents. They've never done anything to discourage me. They're always happy for me and have a word of wisdom if I need it.

But when your sibling is a goddamn superstar, a legend in the making, it's pretty evident that your parents have a favorite child.

And unfortunately, I don't play that role in my family.

It's not that they mean to be neglectful, but my sister, Kathleen, has been special from the start. She's an equestrian champion, bound for the Olympics next summer. I was three when she was born, and she rode a horse for the first time at four years old. I remember being seven, at the same riding school our mother bought both of us kids lessons at, and thinking how fun it was.

What I wasn't privy to was just how natural Kathleen was up there. That the instructor pulled Mom to the side after our second lesson and told her just how much potential my sister had.

From there, Kath took off like lightning. Her practices intensified, and by the time she was five, she was at the riding center three to four times a week, for three hours at a time. My parents would either go together, dragging me along, or take shifts. My sister was ranked regionally, then for the state, and soon nationally.

My entire childhood and teenage years were spent at that riding center, but not because I was actually participating in the activity. I did homework on uncomfortable chairs with the smells of horse and hay around me. My college applications were done on airplanes traveling to other states or countries for Kath's competitions. While my parents were hard on me about grades, Kath dropped out of high school two months into freshman year and got private tutoring because the Olympics were on the horizon.

I guess I couldn't be too sour about it; I got to stay with Amelie and Bevan's families a lot, which made us even greater friends. My life is fine, it's great, it's just …

This feeling of inadequacy, of always being second place, permeates everything I do. It would take a ridiculous display of a temper tantrum to even get my parents to notice me, and the amount of times they missed one of my talent shows or school dances because Kathleen had a competition is too many to count.

I've carried that weight on my back my entire life, and so when something like what happened with Austin last night occurs, I can't help the icy fingers of deficiency that creep around my heart.

"Hey, Mom," I answer, trying to shoo the inadequate feeling from my tone.

"Bonjour, my sweet girl. How you doing this morning?" Mom always greets me in a language she knows I know.

And then I feel guilty for hating on my parents so much in my head. Because they do love me, I know that. It's just ... they love my sister more. Or they care about her accomplishments more.

"It's Saturday morning on a college campus. How do you think I'm feeling?" I chuckle.

It's no secret that college kids party and my parents are pretty cool when it comes to that. Though this morning, I don't have the usual Friday night hangover. It's replaced with the lightness of my heart, beating for the boy upstairs.

"Good night, huh? You sound pretty okay to me." I hear some muffled talking on the other end of the phone, and then Mom yells, "No, the cognac one! She doesn't like the black leather."

"Sorry, sweetheart." Mom's attention is back on our phone call. "We're in Connecticut trying to pick out your sister's new boots."

There is a one-of-a-kind riding supply shop there that Kathleen has visited many times, and Mom usually makes the trip with her. Since the Olympics are coming up this summer, my sister's schedule has intensified. Everything has to be perfect, and my parents will spare no trip or expense.

"Oh, nice. Tell Kath I say hi." My voice loses some of its luster.

"How are classes? You did so well last semester, you think you'll land that UN internship this summer?"

It's nice to know that sometimes they do listen and keep track of what I'm doing. I may be the older sibling, which lends itself to being the more doted upon child, but I'm lucky if Mom and Dad remember I made the Dean's List.

Flipping over onto my stomach, I hear someone rumbling in the kitchen down below. I wonder if it's Austin.

"I'm filling out the paperwork now to apply for the internship, so cross your fingers. Classes are good, and I'm especially loving this Russian literature class I got into. It not only delves into the language, but about how the great novelists impacted it. We also have a new room—"

"What's that, Kath? Oh, crap ... Taya? I have to call you back. They don't have the kind of leather your sister likes, and we may have to custom order. It won't be here in time for next month's qualifiers. I have to go!"

Disappointment floods me as she hangs up the phone.

When I wander down to the kitchen, Bevan and Callum are sitting at the table sipping coffee while Scott flips pancakes.

"Can I get some of those?" I sidle up to him, batting my eyelashes.

He snorts. "You're a mooch. Why am I always cooking for everyone?"

"Because you're the best cook, and I hate to." I grab a mug from the cabinet and throw a green tea bag in it while I warm the teapot.

Austin walks in, his sandy blond hair rumpled from sleep. He's wearing a navy and gold Talcott sweatshirt over gray and navy plaid pajama bottoms, and he looks freaking edible.

"Morning," he croaks, looking a little worse for the wear. "Is anyone as hungover as I am?"

Callum raises a hand and then lays his forehead on the table.

"He puked this morning." Bevan snickers but rubs her boyfriend's back as she bends to coo in his ear.

Well, guess they made up. How long until the next impending blowup?

"Morning." I smile at Austin.

I try not to let my heart flutter or my stomach dip, but damn, it totally doesn't work. *Traitors.*

As for the object of my affection? He barely gives me a passing glance.

Well, guess my organs are now taking a nosedive. I suck in a sharp breath, because this is sophomore homecoming all over again. Does he even realize that we flirted? Was he too drunk and now doesn't even remember? That would be just my fucking luck.

I want to smack myself for being so stupid, for giving in to these childish feelings again. Here I thought this was the start of something, but I'm nothing more than that desperate high schooler trying to get the older popular guy to notice her.

I busy myself around the kitchen, doing everything and nothing at all, as the conversation chugs along around me. At some point, Amelie walks in and touches my shoulder as she passes.

"Were you talking to someone in your sleep?" Am stretches her arms above her head.

"Mom called. Then hung up on me," I deadpan, turning to fill my tea.

Bevan snorts behind me. "What a load of bullshit. Let me guess, Queen Kathleen needed her ass wiped?"

My best friend is not a big fan of my sister, especially

because it means my parents forget about me a lot because of her. As someone with her own stark abandonment issues, Bevan is my biggest defender.

When I turn, Austin's eyes are on me. He regards me with something like guarded curiosity, and I want to flip my middle finger up at him. I don't know why I have the overwhelming urge, but I do.

I want to tell him that no, he isn't the only one who can make me feel like shit, but that seems melodramatic.

So I do what I always do. I suck it up, put a smile on my face, and pretend that everything is fine. Because even though I'm not a priority in anyone's life, and even though my heart is slowly fracturing, I'm always the girl you can count on to hold steady.

If I don't have that attribute assigned to me, then who am I really?

"This is 91.7 WTUB! Welcome back to Division Three Hour with Austin Van Hewitt and Gio Natal."

Gio intros us as our radio show comes back onto the air.

"Welcome back, folks. We're here talking about the batting lineup changes Coach Minger made last week, setting up for some more aggressive hitters on the back end of the order," I say in my radio voice.

I've been told I have a good one, voice for radio, that is.

"Yeah, Austin, we're being told that Nevado is going to be batting clean-up while Oscar Young is being moved to the sixth spot." Gio nods at me and points to a notepad he's holding up.

We transition into spring tennis and then talk opinions about the upcoming football season because there are rumors that Talcott will get a new head coach. Overall, it's a great show, and we sign off after our forty-five-minute time slot with smiles on our faces.

My friend and I walk out of the booth, and I'm riding high. There is nothing I love more than radio and talking sports on the radio. It's random that I fell into it; a love of music and that freshman year feeling of wanting to explore the possibilities of college led me here. But once I walked into this dark studio with all of its weird inhabitants, I knew I was home.

I clap Gio on the back. "Great show. I think I heard Marissa say that we had about three hundred listeners."

For a college radio show about division three sports, that's pretty darn good. We're gaining traction in the area among students and the school's biggest sports fans. As a college town with a sports program that houses athletes who would never go pro, there isn't a huge following. But there are diehard fans, and apparently, they were listening to our show.

"Really? That's gotta be a new record for us. Which is depressing, but we're slowly climbing." My friend laughs and grabs one of the subs that the station caters for us, then sits in a spinning office chair. I join him, forgoing the food, and roll over to a computer terminal.

Though there are crazy hours and mishaps all over the place, working at the radio station has its perks. We get catered food on Tuesdays and Thursdays thanks to the university, and I get a salary as the station manager. I was selected for the job over the summer and had to interview three times with various professors. The extra money is helping with my off campus living situation since Dad has pulled all help in the room and board department.

"I think we can reach even more by the end of the semester."

"Then it's hello, New York City, and talk radio superstardom." Gio rubs his hands together.

The way he says it, like he's so sure it's going to happen, makes my stomach weak. Because for him, it's a no-brainer. He's from New Jersey, about half an hour outside the city, and his family is all for him renting some crappy apartment and pursuing his dream.

Me? I have to sneak around and interview for jobs, then worry myself sick with how I'll ever take them even if I land a position.

"Did you bang that girl you were talking to on Friday night?" Gio asks, mustard dripping onto his chin.

My attention pivots from one thing I'm worrying about to the next—my future career to the girl I've been avoiding but can't get out of my head.

Taya. I haven't spoken to her since the party and then breakfast the next morning. I am still pretty put off by how she spoke to me in the basement, even though it was probably just my own history and defenses making me jump to conclusions.

That look she had on her face when the other girls mentioned her sister and mother ... it has stuck with me. Sadness, a little bit of resentment, that resigned look like she had to settle for something her entire life.

I barely knew what they were talking about or why Taya had sounded so bitter when she talked about her mom hanging up on her, yet I'd never connected to a person more.

Barely knowing her hasn't stopped the constant loop of thoughts in my head about her. It's probably because she lives one floor below me in the same house, and there is this magnetism that has me second guessing if I shouldn't just go down there and kiss her. See what it would be like.

"Nah, I didn't." I wave him off, pretending to look something up, so the conversation ends.

"Damn, she was fucking fine. You mind if I talk to her next time I come over? She's your roomie, right?" Gio's thick black eyebrows wiggle up and down.

"Yes, I mind." I glower at him, and his surprised look has me sidestepping. "Because, uh, she's my roommate. You know? It could get complicated."

Gio looks at me like I'm insane. "If I hooked up with a girl who you're going to live with for, what? Four months? And then could avoid her by not coming to your house? Sounds super complicated, dude."

We both know my quick reaction is not because she's my roommate, but at least he lets it drop.

"Anyway, are we still on for that fantasy baseball draft?" he asks, grabbing another sub.

The guy has the metabolism of a cheetah. When we eat out at Brick Tap, the local burger restaurant in our college town, he can eat three quarter pounders and still be hungry.

"Hell, yeah. I'm going to win this year, I can feel it." I rub my hands together maniacally.

"You are not getting the bowling trophy." He wags his finger.

"Brian is not winning. We have to at least block him from that. If I win, I'll split the pot with you. As long as Brian doesn't win."

We've been playing fantasy baseball together, the four of us, including Evan and then some other buddies we rounded up, since sophomore year. And so far, no one but Brian has won. It's not about the money for me—a two-hundred-dollar cash prize at the end of the season. It's a little about keeping the bowling trophy that is awarded to the winner. Although, next year, whoever wins will have to mail it to the new winner since we'll have graduated and all be living on separate coasts.

But Brian is a ninja when it comes to fantasy sports, and I'm determined to beat him this year.

"I can get in on that action." He nods, polishing off his sandwich.

My stomach grumbles, and it's like his hunger is contagious. I pluck a turkey and cheese off the tray and start to eat.

"All right, I'll talk to you tomorrow. Let me know if I can come over. We'll play video games, I can hit on your hot roommate ..."

"Screw off." I chuckle, only half-joking.

But it does make my mind pivot back to Taya. At some point, I am going to see her with another guy. Right under my nose, in my own temporary house.

Why does that thought make me so pissed off jealous?

The thought, *you've got to be kidding me*, nearly leaves my lips as I walk out the front door.

Because out of the only two people home right now, I'm the one who is blocked in. By Austin.

I was going to head to campus to study in the library since my brain won't properly digest Mandarin prepositions in the warmth of my bed. That is, until I walked outside and saw that Austin's shiny, beautiful car was blocking in my hand-me-down, sputtering mess of a truck.

The last thing I want to do is ask him to move it. But I know that I won't learn this information if I don't go to the library. And I have an oral exam coming up in my Mandarin course, one I need to prepare for. Some languages are easy for me, and I pick them up with no problem. Mandarin isn't one of them.

It's been a busy week with classes, trying to craft the perfect application for the UN internship, and just general college student living. We had our dryer break, so wet clothes have been hung over every surface of the first floor as we wait on the maintenance guy. Our landlord is a prick, and Bevan threw a fit when one of her favorite black sweaters was damaged right before the dryer went kaput.

And now this? Is mercury in retrograde or something?

I realize I'll have to ask him anyway since I planned to go get groceries after the library.

With shaky legs, I walk all the way up the stairs to the attic. I've been up here plenty of times, since the boys used to play video games in Gannon's room. Am and Gannon would hang out up here all the time, and I don't know why it became a hangout spot. We have a full living room downstairs. But that's Gannon for you, bringing the attention around like he was the sun and we were all orbiting him.

It's no wonder my hometown friend was selected to be on a reality show, he has the perfect personality for it. There's no doubt that the boy will be famous, and we've all known it from an early age.

My fist raised, I knock, and my heart stutters as my knuckles tap the wood of the door.

"Yeah?" comes from inside.

With a deep breath, I enter his space.

The large attic room, which is probably the size of my normal living room at home, still looks like Gannon's. Not much has changed aside from a Blink 182 poster and the stack of textbooks on the desk. Gannon wouldn't have been caught dead studying or working on something, which is what Austin is doing on the large cream-colored hand-me-down couch in the center of the room. His bedspread is also different, a hunter green where Gannon used to have tie-dye blue.

"I think you parked me in." I don't bother with small talk.

Honestly, I don't think this guy even wants to talk to me. Because, well, he hasn't in over four days. We see each other in the house, smile or nod, and then move on. He never meets my eyes and barely strikes up a conversation, so I've put a safeguard on my heart.

I shouldn't have expected anything to change. We lived in the same town for years and he never cared to notice me. Now, we've gone to the same college for two years and have never crossed paths. Living in the same house shouldn't change his blissful ignorance of me. I am the dumb one that thought it would have meant something.

Austin begins to rise, patting his sweatpants pockets for his keys. "Oh, shit, sorry. Yeah, I'll come down and move it."

I nod, saying nothing else, and turn on my heel to go. The guy doesn't want to talk to me? Fine. But I'm not getting my hopes up by forming some kind of acquaintance-ship with him.

Footsteps sound on the stairs behind me as we descend together, about five or so stairs apart. I feel Austin's heat behind me, or maybe I just imagine it because the sexual tension that invades my space when I'm near him is palpable. Though, there is no way he's reciprocating that or feeling it, too.

Jesus, I need to move on. I'm going out this weekend and bringing the first boy I'm interested in home with me. Seriously, I need to bang these feelings away. I was fine; I was good. Until the guy moved into my damn house. I've been with other people since getting over my crush on him years ago.

Once we're in the kitchen, I twiddle my thumbs, waiting for Austin to put his stuff on and grab his keys. I should have just studied in my room. This whole experience is too long and too awkward, especially because I'm pretty sure we're both aware he blew me off at that party.

"Where you headed off to?" he asks as he sits down to put his sneakers on.

I stand awkwardly on the other side of the kitchen, by the side door that leads down to the driveway outside.

"To the library. I need to study for my Mandarin course, and unfortunately if I do that here I'll only end up watching another episode of *Succession*."

"I love that show." His head whips up from his shoelaces. "What season are you on?"

"Halfway through season two," I tell him, unsure why I opened this door to conversation in the first place.

"Oh, man, such a great show. Fucked-up family, but great show." He chuckles and shakes his head as he stands and grabs his coat.

"Isn't everyone's family fucked up?" I crack the joke, but it sounds too bitter.

I've been in a funk since that phone call with my family.

Austin stops in his tracks and turns with his hand on the doorknob. "Actually, yeah."

We're too close, and he's staring at me. The house is too quiet. Something is about to happen, and I duck under his arm and wedge my way out the door. I will not read into things with this guy any longer.

We move toward our cars, and I'm about to open my driver's side door when Austin stops me.

"You know, I'm trying to avoid studying." He shuffles a foot on the ground in almost a shy manner.

Shy? Austin Van Hewitt? Who would have thought? It strikes me as a background thought in my mind that I don't actually know much about the guy's personality. I only know the larger-than-life hometown celebrity version of him.

He's not moving toward his car, and I'm too sensitive right now to stand here and do this. I'm not sure what's wrong with me, but I just don't feel like doing this.

"Okay? Well, I'm trying to actually do it, which is why I need you to move your car so I can go to the library."

My voice is pretty bitchy, and I'd like to blame it on the guy leading me on. But he's not doing that, I'm just the one who feels like he is. Which pisses me off even more.

"Taya, I think that ..." Austin seems like he's going to say something heartfelt because he looks down and glances back up.

And when he does, I can see a million emotions running through those mocha eyes. But that changes, and he extends his hand like he's trying to make some point. Whether it's to make a point to himself, or to me, I'm not sure.

"I'd love to spend more time with you. How about I grab us coffees and we go to the library together?"

I'm shocked into silence at the fact that he wants to spend time with me. And suddenly, everything I've been trying to tell myself since the morning after the party just evaporates.

Austin will always be *that* guy for me. The one who can make me weak with one look, who I will throw away all my strength for. We all have that guy, the one who makes us look crazy and desperate and can have us doing headstands when we said we were going to sleep. Each girl has been there in their life, and if you say you haven't, you're lying. I'm not certain what power they wield, these guys, but he has it over me, and I can't say no. Even though I seriously want to.

"Okay. Sure." I shrug before I know what I'm doing.

He flashes me a smile and holds a finger as if to say, *one second*.

While he goes to get his backpack and textbooks, I wait in the driveway, hopelessly trying not to read into what is about to happen and make it a coffee and study date with Austin Van Hewitt.

9

Taya sits across from me at our table on the third floor of the library, and I can't help but sneak glances up at her every once in a while.

Okay, not every once in a while. It's more like every millisecond, and I hope she doesn't notice, but she probably has.

But, Christ, how am I supposed to keep my eyes off her? She's effortless, with those tight black leggings covering her legs. I couldn't stop staring at her ass as we walked into the cafe on campus, the library, and then up the stairs to our table. Her hair is loose and down, and she's wearing these thick-rimmed, cheetah-print glasses she slipped on to study.

I have to stop myself from biting my fist at how fucking sexy she looks in those glasses. Images invade my brain, of me lifting her up and lying her down on the table in front of me. Parting her thighs, coming to settle between them ...

Taya clears her throat; she definitely caught me staring at her, and I quickly divert my gaze to the textbook in front of me.

I don't know what compelled me to ask her for coffee instead of just moving my car. She'd come into my room so sullen, almost like she didn't want to be there. The attitude shift I'd seen in her since that morning in the kitchen after that party was a big contrast from the flirty vibes she'd been giving me before.

And I haven't stopped thinking about her over the past couple of days. I thought I would have since I was turned off by what she said. But the next morning, in the kitchen, my curiosity about Taya North just ignited once more when I overheard her brief conversation with her friends.

So I made a split-second decision and am not regretting it one bit. First, we'd gone to the Rat, the cafe on campus, to get coffees. As we waited in line, I asked Taya about her favorite thing to get. A caramel latte and a pumpkin scone. So I bought her those, and she blushed so hard while quietly thanking me that I think my curiosity turned straight into being enamored.

The drive to and from the house to the cafe and the cafe to the library was spent arguing over music. Taya is a strict hip-hop enthusiast, while I prefer country and classic rock. We agreed that The Beatles are untouchable and that a good Drake song will overrule all else. I can't help but smile as I sit here, because I haven't had a conversation quite like that with a girl in a while.

It's not like I really need to study. Honestly, I was barely doing it at home and I haven't been to the library since freshman year. I'm one of those people who works worse in here than I do in my bed, in my room.

But it's like I can't help myself. So here I am, sitting in the library, pretending to study for a test I don't have, and not-so-secretly creeping on Taya.

"So, Mandarin? That's a hard language, no?" I ask, trying to get the conversation going.

It takes her a minute to look up from the notebook she's writing in, her eyes slowly sweeping to connect to mine. "Uh-huh. It's definitely not as easy as other ones."

"Say something to me," I challenge her, leaning forward on my elbows.

She taps a red polished finger to her chin. The color reminds of the dress she wore to the party the other night.

"*Wǒ xǐhuān nǐ de yǎnjīng de yánsè.*"

I'm utterly impressed with her pronunciation. I can barely speak English on the radio most days.

"And what does that mean?" I can't stop staring at the corner of her mouth that her tongue just darted out to wet.

"See now, why would I tell you that?" She winks, and my balls tighten with flirty anticipation.

I sip my coffee and watch as she stares at the way my Adam's apple bobs when I swallow. "I think you said that you think I'm the hottest guy in here."

Taya blushes, and damn, could I get used to seeing her cheeks go all pink. "I don't even know if that's true, haven't seen all the available options in the library right now."

Neither of us is addressing that I kind of walked away from her at that party. But I know she's cautious because of it. We were drunk, and either of us could use it as an excuse, but I don't think we know each other well enough to actually talk about it. Plus, it's awkward on both sides. What am I going to say? *Well, you mentioned my last name and how I used to act in high school which is a big turnoff for me ...*

Yeah, no. I'll settle for her thinking I'm kind of a jerk, if that's what she thinks. Once we hang out more, she'll see it's not true. And maybe I can determine if she was just drunk and saying shit, or if she's actually like everyone else back in Webton.

"Yeah, I don't think you need to do all that. You know who is sitting across from you." I cross my arms over my chest.

"Maybe I said that I'm sitting at a table with the *cockiest* guy in the library." She chuckles, biting the tip of her tongue where it sticks out.

In the most smug, suggestive moves of all, I look down at my lap and back up at her innocently. "*Maybe.*"

But instead of blushing, Taya throws her head back and laughs. The tinkling, infectious sound sends goose bumps from my shoulders down to my wrists, and my heart does some weird lurch thing.

When she bends forward, clutching her chest and shaking her head, all of those brown waves fall into her face.

As if my arm is mesmerized, it moves to reach out to her. My fingers connect with her cheek, the smooth skin something I want to feel all day. I want to run my hands all over her naked body but will settle for this since there are at least a dozen other people on this floor.

"Your hair is like silk," I murmur, almost to myself.

Taya's dark eyelashes flutter closed, almost kissing her cheeks, and she sucks in a breath. I pull the lock that's shadowing half her face and tuck it behind her ear, my fingertips curving down to the lobe.

"There. Now I can see you." My voice is a whisper.

Hypnotizing hazel eyes blink at me, dazed, and I want to launch myself across the table and fuse my mouth to hers. My cock hardens in my pants as I imagine grabbing her hands and leading her into the stacks. We could get lost in there for a while.

But this time, it's Taya who pulls back. She clears her throat, fumbling her fingers through pages in her textbook.

"We really should get back to studying. I have so much to cram into this brain." Her laugh is nervous and skittering.

Okay, I get the message. I backed off at the party, and now she's the one playing hard to get. That's okay, we can get to know each other, play the long game.

Even if my dick is screaming at me to get the fuck up and get lost in the depths of the library with her.

A nother Saturday night, another party.

College is a bit repetitive in this way, what with us busting our ass all week in classes and then letting loose like animals on the weekend. But it's a cycle that everyone can get behind. These are the crazy years, right? At least they're supposed to be.

Drinking to excess and experimenting with our bodies is the fun part. And tonight, I plan to take part in both. Because I aced my Mandarin exam and I had an unofficial date with the guy I've been crushing on forever. I chalk that up to a pretty good week.

The house is in full swing, and I'm sitting on the kitchen counter with Amelie and Bevan.

"Remember the time we drank gin from that water bottle at the basketball game in high school?" Am cackles.

We're all about four shots deep and feeling like a million bucks. I bop to the song that Scott just put on over the loudspeakers and shimmy my shoulders. Which causes me to almost fall off the counter, and Bevan snorts a laugh at me.

"Oh my God, and Bev nearly puked on the floor! She would

have made some poor varsity player go sliding in her vomit." I clap my hands, remembering the exact moment.

"Not funny! It was the first time Callum and I broke up and I was devastated." She pouts.

"The first of many." Amelie toasts her heartbreak, and I giggle.

"You are the worst friends." She sticks her tongue out at us.

"We're the best, and you know it." I try to kick her, but it just ends up sending me off-kilter, and my heel goes flying across the kitchen.

Scott grabs it, runs over, and places it back on my foot. "Cinderella, your glass slipper."

We all laugh at that, tossing our heads back.

"Who the hell are all these people?" Bevan looks annoyed.

She's the angry drunk who tries to fight other girls if they bump into her.

"Do we care? It's a party, relax." I roll my eyes.

Although, the one person I am looking for hasn't entered my orbit yet.

After our coffee "date," there was some intense flirting going on with Austin. It has been three days, and we are doing this odd mating dance. Circling around each other, coming close, but never quite committing. I feel it in the air, this is going to come to a head. Yes, I've thought that about the first party we had at the house, but this is different. We've spent time together, and he's been the one to pursue it.

Pressing a palm to my chest over my rapidly beating heart, I try to calm the organ.

"Have you found your man yet? I think you just need to drag him upstairs and see if he's packin'," Amelie suggests.

Bevan slurps from her red cup. "I heard from Kimber Teltol that he's big."

"When?" I narrow my eyes, not loving that Kimber has been with him.

"They hooked up the summer before our senior year of high school. She said he's a perfect gentleman." Bevan nods her head.

"Is perfect gentleman code for he made her come first?" Amelie deadpans.

Bevan and I both simultaneously unhinge our jaws, then start hilariously laughing.

"I love how dirty you are when you drink." Bevan hooks an arm around Amelie's neck and pulls her in for a hug.

That's when I spot him just outside of the doorframe to the kitchen. Austin is leaning against the wall, bracing himself with a hand, and a tall, thin redhead is standing with her tits pushed out. Her chest is practically brushing his, and he's whispering in her ear. I can't see his face, but I imagine his eyes full of lust as she runs a purple fingernail down his bicep.

Rage, and something like the cracking of a heart, rings out in my chest. Again, I'm more ticked off at myself than I am with him. Although, no. This time, I am pissed at him. He's the one who brought me for coffee, who wanted to drive me to the library. He's the one who sat across from me and couldn't keep his eyes off me and then brushed my hair behind my ear.

Austin is the one who has been giving off vibes; I'm not crazy. And here he is flirting with some girl in front of me days later, *in my own house*.

It's just like it always has been. I'm cute, but not enough to notice. Not enough to put first or have as his only option, even for the night.

"Oh, fuck this." I hop off the counter, and Bevan and Amelie's eyes follow me.

I hear one of them say, "oh, shit," as I leave the kitchen.

Marching onto the dance floor, I see Landon, a guy I made out with at a Halloween party last year. He'd been a good kisser, wasn't too inappropriate, and is a brunette. I'm not going to get hung up on a brunette since those guys generally aren't my type.

He's going to be it tonight. I am going to take him upstairs and make Austin jealous.

Jeez, I am doing this to make him jealous. Not get off, or have a good time. The alcohol reasons with me and wonders why I can't do both. I can, and I *will*.

Landon is wearing a polo, *oh, God, it's way too preppy*, and I grab the lapels of it. He looks shocked for a moment but then registers it's me and his mouth instantly dives for mine.

I rear my head back, dodging him because, well, do I really want to make out with him?

Instead, I turn into him, grinding my butt to his crotch as the rap beat blares overhead. Landon is uncoordinated at best, and my buzz is starting to wear off. He probably is not that great in bed ...

My thoughts wander, and this idea seems worse with each passing second.

I feel Austin's eyes on me from across the room. The redhead is gone, not attached to his hip anymore, and those chocolate brown eyes are annoyed and taunting.

You're really going to do that? His gaze says.

So stop me, asshole. I raise an eyebrow.

He turns his hands palms forward and shrugs his shoulders as if to wave the white flag. As if he's saying, *if you want to do that, not my problem.*

I hate this. The whole thing. The push and pull he's been giving me since the day he moved into this house. The fact that I'm allowing myself to be so malleable and weak after all these years of inattention.

Landon has begun sucking on my neck, and not in a good way. The flirty buzz, the lustful anticipation I've been feeling all night has completely burned out.

When I look back across the room, Austin is no longer there. I shove off of Landon, who I think yells *what the fuck* at my back, and head for the stairs.

What started out as a night full of possibilities has now dwindled down to none. And I'd rather spend it in bed than facing any more drama downstairs.

"**G**ot it."

My voice is so tight, I can feel the lump forming in my throat.

"I'm serious, Austin. We expect you to make the drive home for the celebration. Your grandfather is retiring, the local newspaper will be here. We need each generation present. Especially you. You'll be the face of the Van Hewitt's in this town someday, and they need to be familiar with you. This is your duty."

As if being some medium-sized suburban town's weird non-mayor is all I've ever wanted. I wish I could reach through the phone and punch my dad. He's a condescending prick on a good day, but today he's in full Lester Van Hewitt mode. Preachy, self-righteous, acting like Webton is London or Paris when really, the Van Hewitt name could disappear and no one would fucking care.

"I told you, I have some radio shows I'm doing that morning and then I'll try to be home." Because going back to my hometown on a Wednesday isn't inconvenient or anything.

"A show about what? Speaking on the radio? Jesus, Austin ..." I hear Dad sigh in his pissed off, haughty tone.

There was no way I am getting into this fight again. How many times over my four years at Talcott has my father, or my family in general, mocked my choice of degree. There have been more fights once I expressed my desire to go into sports radio or broadcasting for a specific team.

If they found out that I was actively searching for jobs to do just that, behind their backs, they'd freak the fuck out.

Which is why I'll placate him and drive all the way to Webton in the middle of the week next month for my grandfather's retirement party. Not that it means much more than formality. The old man will never take his meddling hands out of the business until the day he kicks the bucket.

And now I would have to walk straight into the lion's den. Events where my whole family was present? They are awful, at best. A catastrophe at worst. There is always some family feud going on, with someone not talking to someone. The latest was over my Aunt Mary's will, and three of my uncles were fighting each other for who would get to keep her priceless jewelry collection.

The lot of them are vultures, and I can't stand a single person. Even though he probably would have pitted against each other growing up, sometimes I do wish I had a sibling simply so I could mock everyone in the corner with another person.

"I'll be home that Wednesday."

Angrily, I hang up the phone and throw my cell away from me on the bed. He'll be pissed off that I hung up on him, but right now, I don't care.

Suddenly, the idea of doing this paper on AM/FM theory and the rise of radio in history is so completely unappetizing. Not that it was enthusing to begin with, but now I definitely can't concentrate.

I leave the attic in search of some food or the random beer

on a Monday night. I'm typically not a drinker this early in the week, but I think that phone call warrants one.

The house is quiet, with the roommates out at their nightly activities. I know that Callum and Scott play intramural floor hockey in the fitness center tonight, and Amelie works at the library as a student job and internship for her major. I'm not sure where Bevan is, but I know right where Taya is as I pass the living room.

Pausing because she hasn't seen me yet, I sip on the beer I located in the fridge just before.

It's been about three days since I've truly seen her. She always seems to be coming when I'm going. The other day I asked if she wanted to get coffee at the Sunrise like we did that one morning because I really enjoyed it. And she turned me down. Said she was too busy.

Except, she didn't make eye contact. I wonder if I did something, but have been wracking my brain and can't come up with a thing. I thought something might happen at the party we held the other night, but then I saw her with that guy on the dance floor.

Now is as good a time as any to corner her.

"What are you studying?" I walk into the living room and ask, genuinely curious.

And very turned on as she sucks a lollipop into her mouth.

Taya looks up, clearly not realizing I've come into the living room and seems caught off guard.

"Nuances of the written Arabic language." She blinks.

I snort a laugh. "Sounds enthralling."

"To me it is." She somewhat scowls.

I hold up a hand. "Oh, shit, no, I didn't mean ... I was just teasing."

I always seem to say the wrong shit to this girl.

Then Taya's expression splits into a sly smile. "I'm just fucking with you."

My heart skips a beat. "Oh, jeez, you really got me. Made me feel like a total asshole."

"Don't, it probably is extremely boring to anyone else. But I'm a languages major, and so this is my bread and butter."

She swirls the stick of the lollipop, and I swear a bead of precum drops into my boxers. Fuck, she should not be allowed to so innocently eat that candy.

Taking a seat next to her on the couch, we're now just an arm's length away. "You are? I didn't know that."

Now I feel like a moron for not putting two and two together in the library. Of course, she is, who studies Mandarin for fun? Well, as she said before, I guess Taya does.

"You never asked." She shrugs, those hazel eyes lingering on me.

And there it is, that unspoken unsettling just beneath my skin. There is something she's hiding, and I have a pit in my stomach. I can't put a name as to why, or explain it, but it makes me want to push past her defenses.

"I thought you were just taking Mandarin as a fucked-up challenge or something. Damn. So, tell me now. Why languages?" My arm moves of its own accord, snaking over the back of the couch, and one fingertip grazes a lock of her thick brown strands. I set my beer down on the coffee table with my other hand.

Taya leans in a bit, and instantly the temperature creeps up degree by degree.

"I love how different words in different languages mean the same thing, and then some phrases mean completely different things. In English, we say I miss you. But in French, it's you're missing from me. There is just something so mystifying and magical about translations."

Well, fuck. If that isn't the most beautiful thing I've ever heard come out of someone's mouth, I don't know what is.

Taya is intuitive, thoughtful. She's bubbly and laid-back all at the same time and offers smiles to everyone. She isn't a badass like Bevan or a gumdrop fairy like Amelie. Taya is straight down the middle, the true north. The irony doesn't escape me that her last name is North, and it fits her to a tee.

When I'm with her, I know exactly what I'm going to get. She's witty and knows how to hold a conversation, and I'm learning just how extremely smart and talented she is. Five languages? Who the hell knew five languages?

And goddamn, she's freaking gorgeous. In her natural state, with sweatpants on and her hair piled on her head, I can make out the sun freckles across her nose.

"I'm hoping to add Russian to my repertoire at some point. Maybe if they offer it in whatever job I land."

"You're incredible." It's out of my mouth before I can help it.

I want to look away, but it's the truth, and so I hold her gaze. That is, until she ducks her head and an awkward beat of silence passes.

"Where is your redhead?" Taya asks, never looking up from her notes.

I have to digest the question, and then a lightbulb goes on in my head. So *that's* why she was dancing with some random guy the other night. The guy with no rhythm, might I add. She must have seen me talking to Virginia and made assumptions. Damn, now I'm pissed off even more than I was when I had to talk to my ex-fling. Because it cost me the night I planned to spend exploring Taya in one of our bedrooms.

"Ah, so that's why the random guy," I say first, not explaining myself.

There is that signature blush turning her cheeks scarlet. "I saw you watching."

"Damn right, I was. I wanted that to be me." Honesty is probably best here.

Those eyes, a swirl of chocolate and clover, widen. "What?"

I sigh. "Taya, the girl you obviously saw me talking to was an ... she's not even ex. We hooked up for a month or two last year, and I ended it because she isn't a very nice person. She's always trying to rekindle things, and I was giving her the rundown when you saw me. I've never been as blunt with her as I was two nights ago. And that was because I didn't want anything interfering when I finally went to find you."

"Oh." She swirls that lollipop around in her mouth.

"Yeah, oh." I chuckle and make my move.

I scoot until we're touching. Our thighs. Our arms. Our shoulders.

"Why did we never know each other in high school?" I whisper, my breath leaving traces on her mouth.

Taya stills, her hazel eyes going wide, and I instantly know I said the wrong thing.

"We did." She audibly gulps, pulling the lollipop from her mouth. "You danced with me at homecoming once. My sophomore year. The song was '*Yellow*' by Coldplay. And then it ended and some Pitbull song came on. Katie Miller pulled you away to grind with her. That was the extent of us knowing each other."

That description is not one from someone who casually interacted with me. But my head is in too much of a fog to care, with my lips just inches from hers.

I'm thinking with my cock, which is never a good thing, but I can't help it. We've been skating around this for weeks, and I want a taste.

Bending, I press my mouth to hers. It's gentle at first, a test, and Taya sucks in a breath before sliding her full lips against mine. I taste the watermelon lollipop she was just sucking on, and I want more. I palm her cheeks, the smooth skin sending a zing to my balls, as I move her so I can slant my tongue in.

And fuck, she meets me the instant I enter. The kiss deepens, and I reach down to throw her textbook off her lap. Once it's out of the way, I pull her on top of me. Taya's breasts mold to my pecs through our respective shirts, and I feel her shiver as she presses against me.

But fuck, the girl can kiss. She's grinding on my lap, and I'm so hard I may just bust out of these sweatpants. My hands snake up under the hem of her sweatshirt, and the minute I hit bare skin, we both suck in a breath. Teeth skate over lips; her fingertips are buried in at the root of my hair.

I'm warring with myself in my head. Take her upstairs, or don't. Let this continue, or stop it. I don't want to have these thoughts; I want to be the guy who focuses on only busting a nut and not a damn thing more. But I've never been that guy. I care who I take to bed, which is inconvenient at times even though I know it's an admirable quality. There are more thoughts at play than just getting off, and I can never seem to shut them off.

Which is what has me easing back from Taya.

"Is this a good idea if we're roommates?"

Taya's eyes are dilated with lust, and she shrugs, not making any sort of noise. Am I fucking stupid? This girl is a knockout and clearly would agree to going up to my room right now. I want her so badly that my dick is screaming at me.

But I don't want to fuck up this living situation. I also don't want to lead her on, because a girlfriend is the last thing I'm ready for right now. Especially one who still has two more years of college and is from my hometown. The kind of pressure that puts on me? I'm full up in that department.

"Maybe we should slow it down." I nod to myself as if this is a good thing, what I'm saying.

As if *I'm* not the one who kissed *her*. What the fuck am I doing?

"No, yeah." She nods, tucking her hair behind her ears and scrambling off my lap and back across the couch.

Instantly, I feel cold, lonely, and have a massive case of blue balls—no one to blame but myself. But somewhere in my bones, I know this is the right decision, even if one *boner* is seriously glaring at me.

"But I could stay down here. We could watch *Succession*. You still on season two?" I smile, trying to not-so-obviously rearrange the bulge in my pants.

"Um ... yeah." Her smile is hesitant, and I kind of hate myself for stopping this.

But I mean it. If this is something we're going to do, ending it could mean consequences. I can't afford not to think of those.

Plus, the rest of the night isn't a total bust, no pun intended. We sit on the living room couch and watch a fictional fucked-up family, kind of like my real one.

I get to know Taya more than if I took her up to my bed and learn that I'm becoming even more infatuated with this girl.

12

Somewhere downstairs, a door slams after Callum rattles off a string of expletives.

Three minutes later, Bevan is barging into my room with Amelie hot on her tail.

"I could fucking kill him!" she screams, and I'm sure this is about her toxic relationship.

"I feel like we've been saying this a lot about Callum. Should we just do it already?" I quip, sitting up and making room for them on my bed.

Amelie takes up residence in my desk chair, curling into herself, while Bevan invites herself fully onto one side of my bed.

"He said he doesn't feel like going to the business school dance, so I have to go alone." She pouts, and I can tell she's truly upset.

There are times when their fights are purely stupid. About who left the peanut butter lid off the jar or why Callum didn't fill her car with gas. But this one? I can tell it hurt. Bevan is one of the Talcott Business School investing club leaders, and she loves attending events for it. She honestly doesn't look like the Wall

Street type, but she's whip smart with numbers and is going to be a goddamn shark in that world once we graduate. One of her biggest achievements was being named to the investing club, and Callum hates going to the events. I think it's because he feels out of place, and Callum loves to be the big shot. In that world, he's just dumb. Or at least he sees it that way.

"I'll come with you," I volunteer, even though it's not really my speed.

"Me too. Hey, at least I can flirt with some business majors." Amelie shrugs.

"Oh, are we flirting?" Bevan looks to our petite friend.

"I figure I have to get over this Gannon thing. He's probably not even coming back to school. Either way, I have to live my freaking life. So, flirting with business majors it is."

I nod. "I could get behind that, too. Sign us up, Bev. You'll look all professional and badass, and we can flirt with the future of Wall Street."

"Um, I'm pretty sure you already have a flirt partner. And a damn *fine* one at that." Bevan raises her eyebrows.

"I still can't believe he didn't take you upstairs and go to pound town. We're sure he's straight, right?" Amelie sounds cautious.

"Honestly? I don't know. I can't freaking tell anymore. One second, it's so hot we're practically burning the house down. The next, he's cold as ice and skittering away. Then a day later, he'll ask me to coffee but drop me off before things get too spicy. It's the most confusing thing ever. I feel like I should just let it drop, because how the hell am I supposed to decipher it?"

"You went for coffee yesterday again?" Bevan taps her chin.

This is what we do, and if you're not one of us, you'll never keep up. The subject changes rapidly, from one person to the next or one situation to the next. And we all know what's going on, we can all follow.

"Yes. *UGH*! I mean, the guy kissed me. It was a freaking great kiss! And then he just stopped it. And hasn't kissed me since. I have blue balls."

"Don't talk to me about blue balls," Amelie warns.

The virgin of our friend group. I swear, she's saving herself for Gannon, which is dreamy, romantic, and somewhat admirable, but also stupid as hell because the likelihood of it happening is worse than a snowstorm in Cancun. Both Bevan and I have told her this, but I know she's still holding out hope. She loves him with all of her being, and if it's not the exact right situation outside of the Gannon thing, she won't sleep with someone else.

I worry about my Amelie.

"Sorry." I grimace. "I'm just frustrated. The guy I've had a crush on forever finally notices me, and instead of taking my willing vagina, he's being … respectful? Is that what it is? Damn, I can't believe I'm still pining over this kid."

"If it helps, I'm in love with my best friend who has only ever seen me as a kid sister." Am shrugs, her face clouding with sadness.

"And I'm dating the lunatic I can't seem to get away from because I'm addicted to his toxic ways. God, we're all fucking pathetic. Who would have thought back in high school, when we thought about college, we'd be here? Three strong-ass women pining over these weak fucking men." Bevan collapses onto my pillows.

I am truly confused. Austin is going from hot to cold more times than my coffee does on a morning when I constantly forget about it. In one breath, I thought we were finally headed to the place I've always wanted to be. And then the next, he won't talk to me for a day and acts like everything's platonic when he sees me.

There were so many times, that I decided that I was done

with this in a fit of rage. That I would go find some other guy who would be hanging all over me. But I've tried that with Landon for five seconds, and I hated it. There's something I crave about the chase with Austin, about his inaccessibility and keeping me on my toes.

Bevan's right, we really are fucked up.

Doesn't mean I'm going to give this thing with Austin up, even if I know how much I'll probably get hurt.

13

March first brings an unseasonably warm day, and there are students all over the quad as I walk back to my car.

Most classes are over for the day, aside from the ones that start around dinner time, and the students of Talcott have pounced on the rare above sixty spring day.

Footballs whiz past my head, girls are baring their legs on colorful blankets spread over the grass, and many people enjoy their meal out here instead of in the dining halls.

Sometimes, I miss my days of living on campus. But then I remember that I feel much more like an adult human living in a house on an actual street, not getting my omelet made by a dining hall staff member, and being able to check-in without answering to a resident advisor.

I roll down the windows in my car as I make the ten-minute drive down to the hill to my house, and nod along to Jimmy Buffett all the way there.

After parking, I grab the mail from the box down on the street. I usually check every day because it seems the other housemates aren't so great at it. Maybe because it was my chore during my childhood, to walk down to the street and collect that day's mail, that it's just ingrained now. But the first time I went in there, there were about fifty letters and three packages stuffed into Six Prospect Street's mailbox.

So as I grab it and make my way to the house, I start filing it out into piles for each roommate. Nothing for Bevan. An advertisement for tires for Callum. A letter from the school for Amelie and another for her that looks to be a personal card from her family to her.

Taya has some ads for clothing websites, and Scott got a small Amazon package.

Unlocking the door, I examine the last letter in the pile. Huh? An envelope addressed to the house, sent by Mr. Belding? Mr. Belding was my freshman English teacher in high school.

Then I remember. The time capsule letters. Oh shit, I didn't realize it was time for those, but I guess it makes sense since this is my senior year of college.

Freshman year in that English class, we were supposed to write our thoughts about our lives at that point, anything we wanted to include in it. And then pen some things we wished for the future. I remember writing mine but have no recollection of what I put in there. Now I'm curious to see if this little experiment will bring me any guidance.

So this letter has no name on it, but he must have gotten my new address or something and sent this. I'm glad it made it to me. I could use some words to the wise from my old, naive self.

Tearing open the envelope, I'm actually kind of happy this fell in my lap today. Last night, Dad called me with more less-than-subtle hints that I need to join the family business come May. Of course, it was right before I was about to lounge in bed and fall asleep to some dumb show, and I was restless the whole night after. It's like he knows when I'm trying to relax and has to fuck up the mood.

Pulling the letter out, the spiral notebook paper is a little less white than it would normally be from sitting in an envelope for almost eight years. The minute I start reading, I know this is not my letter.

The handwriting loops and swirls, a pretty cursive that could never be mine.

"Oh, damn ..." I mutter to myself, realizing I was sent the wrong letter.

I hope someone doesn't have mine. They're probably reading my angry fucking thoughts about being a Van Hewitt. That, or my desire to lose my virginity or some other stupid crap I would have been stressing over freshman year of high school.

I shouldn't keep reading, but I do. And then my eyes snag on one thing.

My name.

What?

I hold the paper closer, as if it might give me an answer as to how my name is in this other person's letter.

Someday, I hope that Austin Van Hewitt notices me. I hope he loves me the way I love him. I want to walk around Webton holding his hand, and everyone will know that the perfect boy loves me. He's the cutest, sweetest guy in school, and I just hope he'll love me. Maybe when I'm reading this, we'll be together.

What the actual hell? I'm flabbergasted, standing in the foyer of the house, unable to move my feet. Who's letter is this? And how the hell did I end up with it?

Flipping through the notebook paper—four sheets in total —like a maniac, I look for the signature.

And feel a metaphorical bullet graze my heart when I see just who signed it.

Taya North.

My roommate. The girl I've been flirting with and taking out for coffee. The one I kissed.

My jaw is somewhere on the floor, and my brain races in a thousand different directions. I'm at a loss, and so many emotions swamp me.

Shock, utter shock, that she had written this about me that long ago. Extreme annoyance that she'd viewed me as some Van Hewitt prize to walk around town with. Guilt because I'd never noticed her, and she clearly had felt a certain way about me for a long time. Another heaping ounce of guilt because I'm reading this letter that was meant only for her eyes.

But most of all, I feel duped. Has she been pursuing me for years without my knowledge? Did she make some play with Callum to get me to live here? Has she been slowly pulling me into her web to live out this fantasy?

This is what I meant when I said she didn't speak like someone who had casually been around me growing up. The way she spoke about that homecoming dance? It clicks now.

Fuck, I want to unsee this. Not only am I ... honestly? Creeped out. But I'm invading her privacy. Somewhere in the back of my mind, I know that. Even though I thought the letter was for me, I never should have read this far.

But how could I have known this was in here?

At my back, the sound of the door opening has me jumping. I stuff the letter into the backpack at my feet and jerk to my full height.

"Hey," Amelie says, her kind smile landing on me.

"Uh, hi." I sound jumpy; I know it.

She gives me a strange look. "You okay? I was just going to make myself a peanut butter sandwich. Want to join me?"

She's wearing gym clothes, and a bead of sweat drips from her hairline. I'm sure she just came from the gym.

There is no way I'm about to sit in the kitchen with her. I have no idea what to do with the information I just received and feel epically guilty that I even read through the thing. If I sit across from Taya's best friend, I'm bound to blurt it out.

And the only person who deserves to hear this, and hear it first from me, is Taya. Though the thought sends queasy bile rushing up my throat.

Fuck, this is going to fuck everything we have going up. This is going to fuck my living arrangement up.

But I feel like I have a time bomb in my backpack, and I want to toss that dangerous item into the hands of who it rightly belongs to. Though I know when I do, it's going to explode automatically.

14

Midterms are only two weeks away, and I have to write an entire paper in French for my diplomatic relations course.

Then there is the group presentation for my customs of African nation's course, which I despise. Not the course, it's incredibly fascinating. But the whole idea of group presentations is terrible to me. I'm always the one who does the bulk of the work, and I hate speaking up to argue with others. So instead, I fester in my anger while I earn everyone a stellar grade.

And last but not least, I submitted my application for the UN internship. I won't know if I got it until the week of finals, and I'm so anxious already that I need to calm myself. If I get it, I get to move to New York City in July for a six-week all-intensive languages program that will show the ins and outs of what translators do for the organization.

While I'm trying to figure out how I should carve out each country we've been assigned for the group presentation and how much time to dedicate to their customs, a knock comes on my door. I call for whoever it is to come in.

Austin lets himself in, and my heart skips a beat. Everything comes rushing back from the night he kissed me.

"Hi." I breathe, giving him a flirty smile that I can't help.

Oh my God. The notion that he just walked into my bedroom, after kissing me, hits me square between the thighs. We're alone, in a shut-door room, as he crosses it to sit boldly on my bed.

It's been two days since our last coffee date, and I'm still as confused as I was when I downloaded my feelings to the girls. But here I am, thinking about what we could get up to alone in this room. Bevan's words about being pathetic come echoing back to me,

"Uh ... hey." He rubs the back of his neck and looks mighty nervous. What is going on? "I have to tell you something."

Austin looks around my room with shifty eyes and stares at my desk chair. At first, I think he's going to sit, but then he looks as if he's double-checking himself and thinks better of it. I sit awkwardly on my bed, a pit forming in my stomach.

"See, there was this letter ..." He trails off, looking down at his hands now, where I see an open envelope.

I'm not sure what the hell is going on, but a lump is working its way up my throat. Austin won't look at me, and a sense of dread blankets the room.

You know that feeling you get? That hot-cold, you're about to throw up, sense that something is about to go terribly wrong? Yeah, I have that at this moment.

He hands over the letter, and the minute I see the yellowing notebook paper and my handwriting, my throat goes bone dry.

"What is this?" I ask, my brain playing tricks on itself as I try to stay sane.

Austin looks anywhere but at me, and when he speaks, his voice is so high I want to cringe. "Well, um, I think we had the same English teacher at Webton, and we did those time capsule things. It looks like maybe there was a mix up ..."

He doesn't have to say anymore to get me to understand, and he seems to know it. Which is why he stops talking, and a blush creeps up his neck.

I look down at the papers in my hands, and nausea hurdles from my stomach to my throat. The freshman year letter, the one I was supposed to write to my college self.

"How did you ... where ..." I think my brain is imploding, because I can't form words.

I don't want to look at Austin, but I can't help it. My mouth is open like a fish hanging on a wall, and when I glance up, he's looking at me with a mix of pity and caution. There is also something bordering on anger in there, but I can't digest that right now.

There is no need to ask where the caution is coming from; I know what's written in this letter. My heart and soul die a thousand deaths of embarrassment right here in front of him because now he knows about the epic crush I've harbored for him. Even as a mature, twenty-year-old woman, I feel as small as a middle school girl right now.

I feel like that dorky freshman he never noticed, and one who will never have another chance with him again.

"There was no name on the envelope. I had the same teacher, thought it was mine ..." Austin holds his hands up as if he's playing innocent.

"What you read here ..." My voice is shaky.

Neither of us can complete a sentence; it's all just too painful and awkward. The longer this goes on, him standing in my room like he'd rather be anywhere else, the worse the humiliation is sliding down my neck in hot, pricking waves.

"It's fine. I don't need to know. I just figured I should bring it to you. I'm going to go."

Austin doesn't bother to say another word, and I'm about to dissolve into a fit of hot tears when he finally shuts the door.

Those tears leak from my eyes, staining the paper, and I can't believe what is happening right now. Mortification seals a hot brand on my heart, and I have to clutch my chest to breathe.

As soon as I hear his footsteps disappear up to the attic, I launch myself across the hall to Amelie's room and slam the door closed. Pressing my back and palms to the door as if barricading it from someone, I instruct her shocked face.

"What the hell—" Am starts to address me.

"Text Bevan. Tell her to get her ass up here. We are at DEFCON one." My voice is breathy with unshed tears.

Slowly, my best friend pulls out her phone and texts our other best friend. "Did you finally fuck Austin? Is this what this is about?"

Hearing the word fuck come out of Amelie's mouth breaks whatever spell I'm under. And I start cackling like a maniac. My best friend looks at me even weirder than she was before.

"If only that was the case." I laugh so hard I start to cry, and I'm basically sobbing by the time Bevan comes up.

"What the hell is going on?" she asks, eyeing us both suspiciously. "Why did Amelie text me that we need to hide a dead body?"

Amelie shrugs in my direction. "With the way crazy is acting over there, I figure that's what this is about."

I throw the letter on Amelie's bed and point to it like it might spontaneously combust.

"What's this?" Bev asks, picking it up.

Amelie looks it over as Bev tries to read it and then exclaims, "Wait, is that the letter we wrote in Mr. Belding's class freshman year? I remember those! You got yours already?"

I shake my head like it's about to topple off my neck. "No. No,

I did not. At least I wasn't supposed to. And I'm not the one who opened it."

"What do you mean?" Am cocks her to the side, confused.

"Austin found this first. There is no name on the envelope. He had Belding, too." I nearly scream this, not caring if the guy in the attic can hear me.

A howl works its way up my throat, and I have to stifle it, grabbing one of Amelie's pillows and groaning into it.

"Oh my God, he read this?" Bevan's head shoots up from the letter.

"Well, guess you got to the good part," I grumble, my cheeks growing hot again.

I feel myself start to break down, to dissolve into sobs, and Amelie comes over to wrap me in a hug.

"I'm so freaking embarrassed," I cry to them, and my best friends surround me.

Not only is whatever was happening between Austin and me completely over, but I'm not sure I'll ever recover from this level of humiliation.

15

We had a good ole sleepover to help ease my blues. Amelie on the right side, Bevan on the left, and me in the middle. It's how we've always packed into a bed during sleepovers, unless there was no bed, and in that case, we would huddle together under sleeping bags or blankets.

But I feel a sense of comfort as I wake up, my two best friends on either side of me. It doesn't ease the ache in my heart or the pit of mortification in my stomach, but it helps, marginally.

"Morning," Amelie singsongs, already up and texting on her phone.

"Grr," Bevan grumbles. "Callum texted me last night, from his goddamn room down the hall, annoyed that I wasn't sleeping in his bed. You know this is how much I love you, right?"

She and Callum go back and forth sleeping in each other's rooms, and I don't think they've slept a night apart, besides when they're fighting, since we moved into this house. Actually, I think besides their breakups that only last a few days to a week, they haven't slept without each other since we came to college.

"I love you, too." I roll onto my stomach, on my elbows, and pluck the corner of her eye mask open.

Bevan can't sleep unless it's completely dark, and I bought her this mask a few years ago. It says Queen Bitch on the outside for anyone to read as she sleeps. My surly friend is not a morning person, unlike Amelie, who usually wakes before her alarm. As usual, I'm in the middle, amiable in the a.m. hours but also able to sleep in with the best of them.

"Have I died of embarrassment yet? Because I really feel like I have." I sink my forehead into my palms, as if this might still be a dream I can wake up from.

"Nope. Still with us in the land of the living." Amelie smiles jovially at me.

I flop down on my face and let out a whimper. "I cannot believe this is happening."

"Should we play hooky and just stay here and drink?" Bevan suggests, very out of character for Miss Scholarly.

"As fun as that sounds, I have an exam today and I have to be in class." Amelie gets up and stretches.

"Ugh, me too." I have no idea how I'm supposed to concentrate at a time like this.

"Has he texted you at all?" Am gives me a pitying smile.

I shake my head. I can't pick a worst part of this situation. Is it that Austin knows I had a massive crush on him in high school? Is it the embarrassing words I wrote to describe it? Reading them makes me want to claw my eyes out. Or perhaps it's that he's living in my goddamn house, and I now have to see him every day?

"I doubt he will. He thinks I'm obsessed with him." My throat tightens.

"Well ... weren't you kind of?" Bevan is in a bitchy mood this morning.

"Do you want me to tell Callum all the stuff you wrote in

your notebook about him freshman year?" I glower, feeling bitchy myself.

Her lips form a thin line. "You know, I don't get the whole Van Hewitt obsession. The family is stuffy and snobby. That house of theirs, the one the grandfather lives in? It used to be like a slaughter plant. Fucking gross."

"I'm not enamored by his family." I roll my eyes.

"You kind of sound like it in that letter. Maybe you should explain." Amelie goes over to her dresser and starts to undress.

With the number of times we've seen each other naked, her body might as well be my own.

"Oh yeah, and say what? I'm mortified, Am. The last thing I want to do is come face-to-face with him, much less explain why I wrote that. Jesus, I was fourteen! And dumb. It was puppy love. But what we were doing here, all these years later? That could have been something. Now I'm just ..."

"Sad." Bevan sits up and puts an arm around me. "And that's okay."

Shortly after we have our morning chat, the girls and I are up and at 'em. Amelie is off to an earlier class while Bevan heads to the gym. Scott must have stayed the night somewhere because it's open and empty when I pass his room. Callum isn't anywhere to be found, and I'd know if he was home because the guy is so fucking loud it's insane. Even just walking around, he's heavy on his feet.

I have no idea where Austin is, but hopefully, the universe will let me catch a break and he's already left for the day.

Wandering down to the kitchen, I decide to make myself scrambled eggs and coffee with extra, extra vanilla creamer as a sympathy meal. I put on a playlist, one with rap beats to drown out my thoughts and do my best to lift my mood.

My eggs are bubbling in the pan with the cheese and milk when I hear a door shut upstairs, then footsteps coming down toward the first floor. I literally jump into the air and scurry away into the pantry to hide.

The footsteps slow in the kitchen, and I hold my breath. Dear God, if you have any mercy, you will not let Austin Van Hewitt come in here looking for a snack.

I press my ear to the door, fully aware that I look crazy and my eggs are definitely a burnt mess by now. Whoever it is seems to walk out of the kitchen, and when I hear the front door slam with its signature creak, I let out the breath I was holding.

By the time I make it to the frying pan, my eggs are scorched.

Great. So on top of a burnt breakfast, I'm going to have to sneak around the corners of my house and pray I don't bump into Austin.

Maybe he'll move out, but I'm probably not that lucky. No, I'm going to have to stare my humiliation in the face for the rest of the year.

16

I've been tiptoeing around my house like a goddamn burglar for three days.

And I've never felt more like one than I do now, coming in at two a.m. after my radio shift. My brain is haggard and wiped, I feel like I've been up all night studying, and I was just sitting at the station playing smooth jazz because one of our DJs called out at the last minute.

The house is dark and silent with no trace of life, which is kind of better than me walking in to a lively party, dinner at the big table in the kitchen, or a binge session of a show in the living room.

Because it's been awkward as hell here. I'm assuming the other two girls know, because Bevan has been flipping me off or glaring at me while Amelie is just avoiding me altogether. Callum shook his head and chuckled the other day when I passed him on the way to our shared bathroom. And Scott either doesn't care or is oblivious, but the guy always lives in his own world and is barely home.

Of course, Taya hasn't spoken to me. For the record, I'm avoiding her as well, obviously. I don't even know what to think at this point. I've gone back and forth in my head so many times that I feel like I've been riding around on a permanent roller coaster this week.

One second, I'll think she's just like everyone else in my hometown. A user, a girl after my last name, someone who just wants to claim she slept with a Van Hewitt. And the next, I remember the expression on her face when she realized what that letter said.

It wasn't the face of someone who had been caught red-handed. Taya hadn't looked guilty or like she was trying to hide some kind of intention she had. No, she looked embarrassed. She looked sad. She looked helpless to explain what she'd been thinking. There is a difference there, and I'm not sure I thought about that until now.

Still, I'm defensive. This has been my whole life, trying to keep people away from me who mentioned my last name too much.

But here I am, sneaking around in the dark again. I try not to make too much noise as I unlock the front door and walk in. No one in the living room or the hallway. The downstairs bathroom is empty. Bevan's field hockey stick sits by the bench where we all take our shoes off, and Amelie must have baked something again because the whole first floor smells like cinnamon. Amelie is always baking. As I walk through the dining room, which has most of its furniture moved because of the most recent party, I see Callum's backpack and textbooks all over the floor. Then there is Scott's photography equipment, backdrops, and carrying straps that he leaves in this room. Apparently, he's incredibly talented and barely has to try. From what I know of him, that sounds pretty accurate.

It strikes me that these people are becoming integrated into my life. I've lived with them for over a month now, and I know their habits. I've learned their likes and dislikes, their schedules.

We know each other in ways that no one else will, and it makes us a dysfunctional sort of family.

As I enter the kitchen, the light from the fridge illuminates the room, and I move closer. Bent over so that the most spectacular ass is highlighted in her pink pajama pants, Taya is examining the contents inside. She straightens and plucks a grape out of a bag on the top shelf and then pokes at a Tupperware full of noodles. She removes a cup of yogurt and then thinks better and puts it back.

My lord, but she's beautiful. I only see the slope of her back, the slender curve of her hips, the way her hair whispers down her shoulders as she moves ever so slightly. I remember the way her long, slender legs draped across my lap, her thighs parting as I planted her in a straddle. The way she gyrated on top of me, how I'd gone rock-solid in a second flat.

Blood rushes to the head of my very disappointed dick. I should slink off, go up to the attic, keep up this game of avoiding for as long as I can.

But like usual, when it comes to Taya, I can't help myself.

"I won't tell Bevan you're eating her food if you won't." My voice is low, but she still jumps.

Her body rotates mid-jump until she's looking at me, and she clutches a hand to her chest. "Holy shit, you scared me."

I hold my hands up as if to say sorry. "Didn't mean to. I'm just getting in from the midnight shift at the radio station."

"Isn't the graveyard shift for newbies? I remember my freshman year roommate used to work it and play jazz at three a.m." She scrunches up her nose like that's the worst fate in the world.

I chuckle, because her expression is adorable, but also because I'm not sure how this girl manages to make cute and sexy seem to mesh so well. A pang of confusion passes through me because these are the first words we've exchanged in days, and I somehow miss her. We aren't even an *us*, and yet I miss talking to her. Even after everything I discovered.

"I haven't taken a midnight shift in two years, since I was lowly enough to beg for one. That sounds conceited. Shit." I laugh nervously, because I don't want Taya thinking I'm some asshole who lives up to his family name, the very one I got pissed at her over. "What I mean is, I've paid my dues and earned my right to the prime hours. But as the station manager and lead producer, I also have to pick up the slack should any shift not be filled."

She nods her head. "I get it. The captain goes down with the ship, so you're keeping it from sinking."

"Something like that."

We lapse into an awkward silence, and I'm painfully aware of how quiet the rest of the house is. Taya's expression changes to something between uncomfortable and dejection, and I can see she's about to bolt.

I've been debating seeking her out to talk but haven't been able to get out of my own way. I'm taking this as the universe doing it for me, and I speak before she can run away.

"Listen, Taya, I feel like we should—"

She cuts me off before I can even finish the sentence, though I have no idea where it was going in the first place.

"I don't really want to talk about it, okay? Let's just pretend this never happened. Yeah?"

"It's just, I think we're avoiding each other." I point out, though I don't know why.

Isn't that what I want: to avoid her? I was weirded out by that diatribe for me in her letter, and I should be avoiding her. This is exactly the type of girl from Webton that I don't want to interact with, let alone entertain, having some fun or a relationship with.

"We're housemates, that's it. That's all we have to be. Please, just put me out of my misery and don't talk to me? Talking is the last thing I want to do."

Her eyes beg me, and my chest constricts. Suddenly, I feel like I've been dead wrong about this situation the entire time. Taya looks so small, which is never something I want to make anyone feel. But especially her. She's exposed, vulnerable, and here I've been avoiding her like some idiot who found out a girl liked him and sprinted in the other direction.

I'm just as bad as all those frat guys on campus that I hate.

"I just feel like there is an elephant sitting between us, and I'd like to address it." I try to act like the man I'm supposed to be in a couple of months when college turns into the real world.

"Consider it addressed. I'm embarrassed, you think I'm creepy, and we can lay it to rest. No need to keep up this charade, we both move on. And I'll see you around."

She's talking fast in a hushed tone, as if she's trying not to cry. I watch the way her captivating hazel eyes go shiny with unshed tears.

"I don't think you're creepy at all, I just didn't know what I was reading. It was alarming—"

Taya throws up her hands and snorts out a self-deprecating laugh. "Now, I'm not just embarrassed, but I have to worry about being alarming."

"Shit, no, that's the wrong word, I—" I fucked up with my words, which I tend to do.

Note to self, get better at communicating because you really suck at it. Especially with girls.

Taya backs away, retreating to the stairs. "I get it, Austin. I really do. You won't have to worry about my 'alarming' behavior anymore."

Another interaction gone wrong, I think to myself as I hear her footsteps up the stairs. There seem to be a thousand obstacles when it comes to Taya and me. I just can't quite seem to say anything right to her, and maybe it's for the best that we can't seem to get on the right page.

So why do I feel so distraught and empty standing in this kitchen alone when my heart lit up the minute it saw her standing in the light of the fridge?

Dribble.
    Swish.
        Shuffle. Shuffle.
Dribble. Dribble. Dribble.

I shoot, but the ball hits the backboard and narrowly misses the hoop, bouncing off the rim. The basketball hoop in the driveway of our house is worn and rusty, more of an orange color on the hoop than its original red. The pole anchoring it to the ground has flecked paint coming off of it, and the backboard has black slashes all across it from being dinged a thousand times.

But I still come out here to shoot. Especially if it's warm. There is something that takes you out of your head when shooting around outside, a calm that the big courts in the loud fitness center can't give. When I need to think, I come out and shoot baskets, making some, missing others.

I'm no Kathleen, but I made varsity as a sophomore. I even got my letterman jacket—not that Mom and Dad were around to take me to the ceremony. I'd gone with Bevan and her family when she lettered for field hockey.

My mood is sullen today, because I haven't heard from my family in a week and a half. It's like I came to college and that was their out, their thumbs-up to forget about me. Whenever I call my mom now, it's like she's annoyed to hear from me. I'll tell her about the hot gossip or something funny that happened in one of my classes, and all I get back is an *okay* or *sounds great*. Most of the time, I just feel like she isn't listening at all.

It's a hard pill to swallow, knowing your mother doesn't really care about you. I try to look at the people in my life who love me unconditionally, namely Bevan and Amelie. They're the closest thing to family and real sisters that I have.

Kathleen and I were never close. Maybe when we were little, before the really competitive stages of her equestrian training, but I don't remember that time. She was so focused on her competitions that she barely even noticed I was around. And Kath was …

Well, my sister is one of those people who understands horses more than she understands humans. There's just nothing we connected on, and after a while, we stopped trying.

So I'm out here, avoiding the major issues weighing on my soul and tossing up a basketball instead. I should probably be in therapy. No, not probably. Definitely. But I'm a broke college student who treats my hefty emotional baggage with alcohol instead, just like everyone else around here.

That's what I do these days. I avoid. And Austin Van Hewitt is bullet number one I'm trying to dodge.

After our disaster in the kitchen, Austin tried to approach me once more. It was the day after when we were both home, and everyone was cooking their individual lunches in the kitchen. I pretended I had a FaceTime meeting for a group project and scampered up the stairs. I was so mad I missed out on Amelie's grilled cheese, but there was no way I was staying down there with him.

Not after he called me alarming.

God, just thinking about all of the embarrassing shit he probably thought about me makes me blush and want to dry heave at the same time. Every time I think about the fact that he read that letter, my soul dies a little bit. And I can't even enjoy the silly time capsule letter I wrote because I can't bring myself to read it. What should have been a fun little trip down memory lane is now this shameful, burning secret.

I dribble the ball harder, launching it at the hoop, and it miraculously goes in. At least I can still do something right.

"I didn't realize anyone actually used this hoop." Austin appears on the front porch in gray sweatpants that are innocent but far too sexy to be legal.

His hair has grown a bit shaggy, and I want to run my fingers through the long blond streaks, and there is a smattering of hair on his jaw. It's a bit darker than the style on his scalp, and it makes me wonder if there is any on his stomach, running down past the waistband of those gray sweatpants ...

Woah. I clearly need to get laid. Or be less pathetic. The fact that I'm still having fairly vivid sexual dreams about a guy who called me alarming really speaks to my mental state.

"I come out sometimes to shoot around and think," I tell him, turning my back.

Please go inside, please go inside, I chant in my head.

"I miss a good old outside hoop. Shooting around in my driveway at home is my favorite pastime." Austin's voice comes closer as he talks, and I know he's walked down the porch steps and onto the driveway.

"It's the best," I agree, nodding but refusing to look at him.

Every time I think about this guy, my face turns beet red with shame. I can't believe a person I was so into, had real feelings for, knows my innermost embarrassing thoughts. This is every girl's worst nightmare, and I *live* with him. There is literally no way I can escape seeing him.

"Want to play HORSE?" He raises one thick blond eyebrow in challenge.

Austin towers over me; there is a reason he was the guard on our high school men's basketball team. I know I have some skills on the court, but there is no way I'll win in a trick-shot contest against him. Do I really need another failure when it comes to this guy?

"Nah, I'm good." I pass him the ball on a bounce, and he picks right up where I left off dribbling. "You can play."

I turn to head inside, and his hand on my elbow stops me. It's the first time he's touched me in weeks, and I can't help but stutter-step and shut my eyes. My breathing changes, becoming shallow and cautious. Just the whisper of his fingertips on my skin makes embers burn low in my belly, and I can't control the way my heart smashes against my rib cage.

His dark blond eyelashes flutter closed, as if he can't handle the fragile connection we have right now either. I watch the tic move through his jaw, and for one moment, I think he's going to pull me flush against him and dip down to take my mouth.

But he doesn't.

"Taya. Stay. I want to play with you, it's why I came out."

His confession ignites a flicker of hope in my chest and also makes me weary. Per usual, Austin is jerking me around. When am I going to stand up and stop letting him have all the power here? Will there come a day when I say no more and refuse to participate in this?

If there is, it's not today. Because he's too close, and he's touching me. And I've had this fantasy before, of us playing basketball. It ended with us in the grass, him on top of me, moving over me.

I close my eyes, pushing out all of the doubts, insecurities, false hopes, and whatever delusions I'm still holding on to. I can stay here; I can play the game. It won't affect me.

Yeah right, a little voice whispers in my head.

In the next breath, Austin stops touching me, and I feel like the rug has been pulled out from under me. I miss that light pressure of his fingers on my elbow. I want to know how his hands would feel all over me. I've thought about it for so long, and dammit, I just want to know.

"I'm pretty damn good at HORSE." Mentally, I pull on my armor, allowing me to joke and be the *cool girl* with Austin.

"But not as good as me," he boasts, dribbling the ball with ease. There is something about watching him, his hips loose and moving with the motion of the ball, the way his big hands handle it effortlessly ...

I'm definitely wet. Yep. Need to change my underwear.

"If you win, you can make me do whatever you want." He throws out a gauntlet.

The way his arm muscles tense and constrict whenever the orange leather slides off his fingertips is distracting.

"Like not talk to me for the entirety of you living here?" I give him a saccharine smile.

"Good one." He winks. Is there anything this guy can do that I won't find attractive?

"And if you win?" I dare to ask.

The smug asshole actually smirks. "I get to kiss you."

And my stomach bottoms out. "Austin ..."

My voice is all caution, a warning issued for him not to fuck with me.

"Taya. Just trust me."

Just how am I supposed to do that? I want to ask.

We begin playing, the first two shots an easy sinker from the foul line. Austin is all grace and beauty when he plays, and I catch a glimpse of his abs when he reaches up to shoot. As I move to make him gain an *O*, pun not intended, I feel his eyes tracking my ass in the black yoga pants covering my legs from the right side of the court.

This game is a special form of torture. Foreplay that I'm sure will lead nowhere.

I sink my shot, and then Austin follows suit. We both make it, so no one has a letter yet. Austin backs up to almost the back of the driveway, onto the grass, and then turns around. Shit, he's going to throw it over his shoulder without looking.

As if he has eyes in the back of his head, the bastard shoots and scores, chuckling under his breath. "Think you can make that?"

I sashay past him, careful not to touch him but pass just close enough to hear his intake of breath as the heat of my skin warms his.

"Watch me, jerk," I glower.

Except the nerves in my stomach clank together like dishes in a clumsy waiter's arms. And when I throw it over my shoulder blind, I know it's not going in.

I earn my first letter, an *H*.

Two more rounds and we're both tied with the first letter after Austin narrowly misses the shot I take from behind the basket. It was pure luck that I made it, and even luckier that he missed.

The game continues without us talking, but we're circling around each other like animals performing a mating ritual. My skin is hot and itchy by the time I'm able to make any of my shots, because Austin insists on walking the ball over instead of just bouncing or dribbling it to me. He always insists on touching my hand as he gives the ball to me, or bumping my elbow with his, or catching the ends of my hair on his fingertips.

I miss a shot and add an *O* to my tally. Then I make the next and miss the next two. There is only one letter left, I'm one mistake away from being the loser, and my stomach does a nose-dive thinking about Austin's lips on mine again.

"I'm about to win." He smirks at me.

Something in my resolve, the poker face I've held this whole game, breaks.

"Why are you doing this to me?" I ask, my voice cracking.

He might not know exactly what I'm talking about, but he read the letter. He knows how I felt then. The crush I've carried. Is he leading me on? Is he trying to see how far I'll go on the feelings I had as a teenage girl? Does he just want to fuck with me because he's bored during his senior year?

Austin's face falls from the cocky, competitive grin he's had while we've been playing. "Taya, I'm not trying to do anything."

"One day you're acting like I'm radioactive after you read a letter that was meant only for my eyes. And the next, you're out here trying to kiss me? Sorry, if that's a little confusing for a person, *Austin*."

I think he sees the error in his ways. "I never meant to ... I'm sorry."

The ball falls from my hands, bounces across the driveway, and comes to a stop. "You know what? I forfeit. Which means no one wins. I'll ..."

I'm about to say see you later, but I'm not sure my confidence can handle that. If anything, this little game just fucked me up more.

I hear Austin calling my name as I walk up the porch steps and back into the house, but I don't turn around. We've had enough confrontation for the day.

Imagine if he won, and I let him kiss me. Would I be even more hopelessly gone over him than I am right now?

Brian hulks on at my side, practically moving the ground we walk on, as we stroll through campus.

"I can't wait until it's warm enough so the girls are out in bikinis." He smirks a devilish grin to himself.

"You're a pervert. Those are freshman you're talking about." Since most of the upperclassmen now lived off campus.

"Exactly." Another devilish grin.

I roll my eyes, just happy that it's getting warmer. "I'm just trying to get a smoothie."

We're on our way to the smoothie hut on campus, a frequent spot for every student when the weather in Upstate New York finally begins to creep up past forty degrees.

"Yo." Gio walks up, giving both of us a fist pound, and we all fall into step. "Evan!"

Our fourth friend joins us, and then we're all walking through campus together. I'll miss this when we graduate; passing through the quad with them and just shooting the shit. There is an ease and lack of responsibility at moments like this that I know I'll crave once the real world takes hold of me. I try to remember that as Brian and Evan discuss the twins they took home two nights ago.

"They were freaky as hell. Wanted to go down on us in the same room." Evan laughs, high-fiving our football bro buddy.

"Damn, that's kind of hot, though. Does that make you Eskimo brothers?" Gio ponders, tapping a finger to his chin.

"Nah, we'd have to have swapped their mouths for that." Evan chuckles.

"You guys ..." I shake my head.

"We know, captain of the prude squad. We get it. But you should try it sometime. Have a little fun, let that Hemsworth hair down." Brian slaps me on the back.

The running joke between my friends is that I'm as vanilla as they come. Because I wouldn't bring multiple girls back to our shared dorm rooms in one week or let a chick give me head in the bathroom of a house party.

Little do they know, sex is better when it's not an exhibitionist sport. When you can lock a bedroom door, get a girl you admire or care for on her back, underneath you, and have hours to explore ...

That's the *good* part. And when I get that, there is nothing vanilla about me.

"I've got my eyes on someone." I smirk.

They don't need to know I've royally fucked up the Taya situation because I hope to remedy it. I don't know when I made the switch from being freaked out about potentially dating a Webton girl, and one who wrote so candidly about my last name in her time capsule letter, but I've switched. That little basketball competition was the slowest round of foreplay I've ever had, and I've jacked off the last two nights since just thinking about touching Taya's elbow. Her fucking elbow.

I don't know, either, what was running through my head the other night when I taunted her so much. Maybe I wanted her to crack, but the way she did had left me alone outside on the driveway. I've been trying to make amends or just talk about the letter or what's going on between us. I'm not the type of guy who wants bad blood out in the world, and I feel guilty, strange, *weird* about the elephant sitting on the roof of our house. It's clear she doesn't want to talk about it, so I thought the game of HORSE would be a good icebreaker. Though it seems to have added more baggage to our pile.

"His roommate." Gio chuckles in the direction of the other guys. "But hey, she's a fucking dime."

"Don't call her that." I scowl at him.

"Why is that bad?" Brian gives me an eye roll. "He's calling her a ten, you should be happy about that."

"Because I know what he does. No sniffing around Taya." I wag a finger at him.

"Isn't that her? Because you may want to tell that guy the same thing." Evan points across the quad, and sure enough, Taya is sitting on the grass with another guy.

They're laughing, and she touches his arm.

My blood goes from stagnant to a simmer. I've never been the jealous type; hell, I've barely been the type to want to date a girl. I've had a month's-long relationship here or there, but I've never told anyone I love them. It's never been that serious for me.

Yet here is this girl who defies everything I've said I want in a real relationship, and I'm sure my cheeks are green with jealousy as she sits on the grass with another guy.

Without another word to the guys, I cross the quad, coming to stand in front of where they're sitting. The guy is smaller than I am, dark-haired, with thick-rimmed black glasses, and I try to reach my full height by rolling my shoulders back and puffing out my chest. I've never been this guy, but she won't even give me the time of day anymore, and he's sitting here eating ... cookies with her?

Chocolate chip cookies lay in a Tupperware on her backpack, and their laptops are sitting idly on the lawn.

"Taya, hey." I smile down at her.

She blinks up, the sun in her eyes, and shields them with her hands so I can't quite make out her expression.

"Au-Austin ... hey," she stutters, surprised to see me.

The guy sitting with her doesn't say anything, just blinks at me through his glasses, and then looks to Taya.

I extend my hand. "I'm Austin, Taya's—"

"Roommate. He's my roommate." The words rush out of her mouth.

What the hell? Did she think I was going to be a metaphorical dog and piss all over my territory by calling her my girl or something? Wait, hadn't the thought crossed my mind, though?

"Can I talk to you?" My head cocks to the side, and my voice takes on a pitch of annoyance.

Like I'm frustrated that she's sitting here laughing with him and won't even let me play basketball with her. Shit, I'm a fucking schoolyard little boy right now.

"We're in the middle of studying." She's trying to turn me down or get me to go away.

"I know, it'll only take a second." I put on my most charming smile.

Taya barely blinks at it, and I miss that blush I used to put on her cheeks.

"You know, I have to use the bathroom anyway. I'll be right back." The guy she hasn't even introduced me to gets to his feet and smiles as he goes to duck into one of the buildings.

Taya lets out a frustrated sigh. "What do you want?"

"Wow, so that's what you think of me now." I try to joke, but it lands flat when her expression doesn't change from the annoyed, shuttered look she's giving me.

"I wanted to apologize for the other day. The basketball game. I was dumb to put those stakes on it when we haven't truly talked. It's just, you won't let me near you, and—"

"Well, you think I'm so alarming, so ..." The pain in her eyes guts me.

"Shit, I didn't mean that. It was the wrong word to use, and I'm sorry I was a dumbass for saying it. I just wish we could really sit down and hash this out."

Because if we did and got all the miscommunication out of the way, I think this could be something. But I don't jump right in and tell her that.

"Austin." She shakes her head. "Why? You didn't even want to do ... whatever *this* is"—her hand moves back and forth in the air between us—"before you opened a letter you never should have read. You stopped the kiss we had, you were hot and cold about whether you want to flirt with me or hang out. Now it's ten times more complicated and you want to have some therapy session about it?"

My heart rate speeds up, because she's calling me out for very valid reasons.

"I never meant to make you feel that way, I was just confused about what I want. And then I found that letter, and your words were—"

"I'm not that girl, Austin. That girl was a freshman in high school, infatuated with the idea that a junior guy was hot. I didn't even know you. I knew the idea of you. You can't fault me for that. It's like you having a crush on Mariah Carey, or whoever was your celebrity love interest, when you were eight. I'm incredibly embarrassed about this, and you're making it worse. Why did you even read that letter once you realized it wasn't yours? You had to have known, the minute you opened it up, that it wasn't your handwriting. Maybe I should be pissed off at you for invading my privacy!"

Apparently, the dam has broken, and Taya is letting all of the things she hasn't said to me just flow on out. Part of me must know to shut my mouth, because I don't even try to interject as she keeps going.

"Do I think you're hot? Of course. I've been flirting with you and kissing you and trying to get to know you. Actually *know* you. I wrote that letter six years ago. I was fourteen! You don't think I've matured a bit since then?"

People are beginning to stare at us on the quad, but I don't really care. I won't see ninety-nine percent of these people ever again, and I've been waiting to have this conversation. I didn't realize it would be a tongue lashing, but I'm at least a little glad we're hashing it out.

"Taya, I'm a Van Hewitt. I know what that means to everyone from Webton, but no one knows what that means from inside the family. No one knows what it means from the inside perspective. It means I have to be skeptical of every single person who comes into my life. Do you know how many times I've been used because of my last name?"

Taya is ready to fire back, and I don't even get to make my point about not caring about that letter anymore.

"As far as I'm concerned, I never truly followed through with my master plan, did I? There was no evil conspiracy to make you marry me as a sixteen-year-old kid. Unless you think I mastermind this entire thing. Yes, I definitely made Callum and Gannon invite you to sublet when I didn't even realize it was happening. Oh, and maybe I was the one who made your other situation unlivable, because I'm such a genius!"

She throws her hands up in the air and rolls her eyes, but she's not done.

"You only want me now because I'm so mortified that I can't even look at you most of the time. God, you guys are all the same. I have a crush, want to get to know you, pursue something, but holy shit I'm being too forward. Though, now that I won't let you apologize or kiss me because of some stupid bet, the envy monster in you comes out and you can't stand to be without me? Bullshit. That's bullshit, Austin."

I hang my head, knowing that this is not going anywhere. Not only is she completely done entertaining a flirtation with me, but I've made my living situation completely awkward. Why the hell do I always seem to fuck everything up?

"I'm sorry. I'm really sorry, Taya. I wish I'd handled this better, and you should know that you're the most genuine, unique woman I've ever met."

I wish there was anything to remedy this, but we've both pretty much done all the damage we can. I look away from her, trying to grasp on to anything that might save this, and see her guy friend walking back.

"Nothing else? Great. You can go. I'm not going to be the one to storm off this time, I'm over this."

Those last three words slice deeper than I think she intends them to. Maybe she's right, I only want this when it's a game, a competition to be won. Though, I've never been that guy. I'm just a confused human being who has been controlled and bossed around his whole life. When I'm allowed to make my own choices, I typically screw them up.

Rising and wiping the grass off my palms and onto my jeans, I look down at her one last time. "I really am truly sorry. I'm the one that fucked up here. If you want me to move out ..."

I don't get to get the question out before her guy friend

comes back, and Taya sends me a warning look. She doesn't want him to know what we were just arguing about.

My friends are long gone, probably not wanting to hear about my chick drama and only wanting to joke about their hookups. So, I walk through campus alone, feeling fully dejected.

19

There are parties at the Prospect Street house almost every night of the weekend.

I'm just not at them. After the time capsule letter and the subsequent follow-ups with Taya, I thought it would be good to give us our own territories while trying to have fun. And since I didn't feel like staying at the house and watching her flirt with guys because *that* made my blood boil, I did what every other twenty-one-year-old at Talcott does.

Go to the bars.

There are three main bars in the Commons that college students frequent, but the night always ends at Stars Bar, where there's a large dance floor and stage most of the girls drunkenly climb on by the end of the night. I've spent the last two weekends at Stars, because I couldn't go home until I was sure most everyone was asleep.

Especially Taya. It's easy enough to avoid her during the week, since we seem to be sticking to our opposite corners, aka our rooms. But when the roommates throw parties every other Friday and Saturday night, it's inevitable I might run into her on the way up to the attic.

But tonight, I'm drunk and feeling sorry for myself. The past two weeks have sucked. Even though the thing between Taya and me was just blossoming, I miss talking to her. She has a great sense of humor, and our conversations were always something I looked forward to. She's also sexy as hell, and it's damn difficult to keep myself from staring at her when I catch her in the kitchen in her pajamas.

I don't feel like being at Stars; every obnoxious drunk person, loudmouth girl, and overly cocky guy is pissing me off. The music choices are terrible, and the whiskey is hitting me in the wrong way. Instead of a happy buzz, I'm in that sullen, wasted mood that only leads to a fist in the face if someone touches me the wrong way.

Waving to Brian and the guys, I walk out of the bar alone. Six Prospect Street is in sight, so it's not like I'm in danger. My sublet house is just a few yards from the Commons, which I guess is good on a night like this.

The music filters out onto the street from five houses away, and I know I'm about to walk into a huge rager in the house. I make it to the lawn, and there is already one kid throwing up out here and a couple half-naked humping each other in plain sight. Ah, college, the definition of class and propriety.

Our front door is fully open, inviting anyone in, and there are people *everywhere*. Maybe I'm just surly and drunk, or maybe this party is bigger than the others I've attended here, but it seems like I can't breathe or move a square inch with how many people are packed in here.

When I finally make it to the stairs, I find Bevan straddling Callum's lap on the midway landing. They're making out and dry-humping like there aren't three hundred people in our house, and I assume they're back *on* rather than screaming bloody murder at each other.

My mood dampens when I make it to the second floor and

realize I never saw Taya. Is she with someone? Has she already gone up to her room with another guy? My attitude turns even more sour.

I'm about to head up to the attic when a door in the hallway opens, and as if put there by fate, out comes Taya.

Fucking hell. She's wearing a scrap of a dress, almost the same color as her skin and smooth silk. She looks naked, and I'm instantly hard as a steel pipe.

Her eyes collide with mine, and she looks like she's about to turn on her heel and retreat to whatever room is open and unoccupied.

But I'm quicker. Something in me snaps, and I can't stand this anymore. While I'm still freaked about what I read in there, I can't stay away from her. And the way she's been avoiding me, not talking to me, suddenly pisses me off.

My breaking point is reached, probably by the help of the two four-finger pours of whiskey I had at the bar, and I'm on her in a second.

"You going to run away from me every time you see me now?"

"Austin." Her voice is a snide remark and a warning.

"I said, are you going to bolt each time I walk into a room now? I'm fucking tired of you avoiding me."

"And here I thought you would rather me stay away from you. Aren't I just so alarming?" She throws my words back at me.

We're both drunk and irrational and spewing whatever animosity has been trapped inside.

I walk toward her, and she backs up until her back hits the wall. My hand comes to her throat, gently holding her there, and I feel the gasp work its way up the column of her neck. Her pretty hazel eyes dilate, and my hold on her neck tightens a fraction as I press my nose to her cheek and run it up and down that bone I love to make blush.

"Am I setting off your alarms now? Do you want me to, what did you say on the quad the other day? Go now?" I'm being an asshole, but the combination of my mood and her downright rejection of me the last few weeks have me in a tailspin.

Taya is right. She was a fourteen-year-old with a daydream and a crush and wrote some silly diatribe to a boy she didn't even know. I'm punishing her for my own fears and doubts about how people view me or how they've always treated me in my hometown. This drop-dead gorgeous woman standing in front of me is self-aware, sure of herself, and so fucking sexy in her confidence and demeanor that I'm not sure what the fuck has been wrong with me this whole time.

Holding her to what she wrote would be like holding me to the epic crush I had on Vanessa Hudgens as a kid. I plastered her posters all over my room and watched her scenes of *High School Musical* more times than I can count. Would I be embarrassed to ever meet her in person and have her find out that I cut out pictures of her and put them on my dresser, thinking about what we'd look like as boyfriend and girlfriend? Hell, yes. And I'd also be humiliated if she ever called me out for it.

It's at this moment that I realize I've invaded Taya's privacy on such a deep level. Then I took it and twisted it into something wrong, something shameful.

Fuck, I'm the asshole in this situation. Thanks for pointing it out, Vanessa Hudgens.

"Are you going to kiss me, or chicken out again? Because so far, your bark is worse than your—"

I swallow her words, pressing my mouth to hers so ferociously that it takes her a minute to catch up. My tongue invades her mouth, our teeth and lips colliding. Every pent-up smidge of desire I've held at bay crashes out of my body and into hers. Taya is giving as good as she gets, her hand cupping me over my jeans and stroking my cock. Thrusting my hips forward, I can't wait any longer.

Hauling her up with a growl, those long legs wrap around my waist, and this time, it'll take a fucking crowbar to separate us. I'm not stopping anything, and I'll show her just how satisfying my bite is.

"*Austin.*" She grinds her center into me with each step I take up the stairs to the attic.

I want her in my zone, on the top floor, where no one can interrupt us. The party rages below us, the beat of the music filtering up to the third floor, but we're alone in the dark, and I've never been more ready.

I set her down, our bodies still molded together, as we grind and kiss and feel *everywhere*. Our hands are moving at hyperspeed, trying to touch each inch while being distracted by the next.

The roughness of the fabric has to be creating a maddening friction against her clit, because she's clawing at me as I back her up into the room.

"Austin!" she yelps when I push her panties to the side and push a thick finger inside her.

This is going to be loud; we're going to be loud. The music downstairs will drown us out, but I don't give a fuck. Even if this house were completely silent and full of people, I wouldn't hold back. I want all of Taya's fury and fire.

And goddamn, do I love it when she says my name. "Keep saying my name, beautiful."

My lips spark a trail of fire down her neck, pushing at the thin material of her dress as she wiggles against me and the finger inside her. One second we're standing, and the next, we're in free fall as Taya pulls me with her as she lands with a thump on the bed.

"It only has to be once. I have to know," she whispers, almost to herself.

As if this will ever just be a one-time thing. I'm not even inside her, and I know I'll never get enough.

"Then take your fucking clothes off." My temper spikes because she's dead wrong if she thinks we won't do this again.

Hazel orbs flare with desire when I curse, and when Taya just lies there and pants, I reach under her and pull what she's wearing clear over her head. The only thing left is a lace thong, the one I just pushed away to finger her, and I can smell how soaking wet she is. She kicks her heels somewhere into the depths of the attic, and I pull the panties down her hips.

In seconds, I'm crawling down her body and then my tongue is inside her folds, lapping at the sweet wetness glistening on her skin.

"Fuck!" she cries out when I push a finger inside at the same time I suck on her clit.

Her hips buck off the bed, and this might be my new favorite drink. Fuck liquor or beer, I'm going to get drunk off Taya.

Delicate but demanding fingers are pulling at my shirt until it's up around my chin, my head in her pussy obstructing the material from pulling free of my body. I lift so Taya can pull it all the way off, and she takes advantage of the position by undoing my belt buckle. Just the sound of that makes my dick twitch with immense anticipation.

"I want you. *Now*."

She doesn't have to tell me twice. In a flash, I'm naked and reaching to my bedside drawer for a condom. My dick is so hard that the minute it meets the air, I'm hissing. Taya takes it in her hand as I rip open the condom with my teeth, rubbing her thumb over the pre-cum leaking out of my head.

I nearly swallow my tongue when she touches me, and I'm about to blackout as I roll the protection on and position myself.

When I push in, we both groan so loudly it must wake the gods. I don't know how long it's been for her, but it's been too long for me. Too long and too much waiting when it comes to this woman. The sense of relief is just as heightened as the sense of pleasure.

This is why I wait. This is why I assess and don't just fuck every random girl. This is why my friends think I'm a prude who can't get down with a little kink.

Because when I finally connect with someone and it gets physical, the chemistry is out of this world. As I skate my teeth over Taya's bare skin, I feel like the entire world could implode, and the two of us would still be here. We're going to fuck each other's brains out, and it'll be the hottest thing anyone could ever experience. This is better than twins giving blow jobs or threesomes with nameless faces.

There is nothing better than Taya under me right now, clawing at my back as I press her knee back into the mattress. There is nothing better than the look on her face when I thrust deep, making her eyes roll back. There is nothing better than the sounds she's making or the way her teeth have sunk into my shoulder.

And there is definitely nothing better than pounding into her with wild abandon before feeling her pussy spasm and the guttural moan leave her throat as she orgasms.

I swear to all that is holy, I could die a happy man right here, right now.

I'm a predatory animal, drawn to the smell, sight, and sound of her as she gyrates her hips up into me and milks that orgasm for every last drop. I'm so enthralled that I don't even realize I'm about to come until white spots dot my vision and my whole body seizes in rigors of lust and pleasure. The growl I let out surely just shook the whole attic, and I bury myself in all of her chocolate brown waves as I spill into the condom.

Catching my breath is hard as I come to my senses, Taya still wrapped around me. I roll to my side, careful not to put my weight on her, and pull her against my chest. We don't speak, the intense reality of what just happened floating all around us.

I want to do it again. Immediately.

But Taya pushes off and rolls away.

"Where do you think you're going?" I ask, some of the venom from my mood tonight still trapped in my chest.

"It was just once." Her voice is small and quiet.

My fingers circle her wrist and pull her back down until I can climb over her and I'm positioned between her legs again. My cock is already getting hard, the head pressing on the inner part of her thigh.

"If you think that, you're truly insane."

"Or maybe you are, for bringing me up here."

She's always challenging me, and I kind of love it. "Let's find out whose crazy then."

"You're late."

It's the first thing Austin's grandfather says when he greets him, and I get the vibe that this whole affair is going to be awkward.

When Austin asked me to drive up to Webton in the middle of the week, I was pretty shocked. We were sitting at the kitchen table eating lunch together, he'd surprised me and picked up subs from a place I liked in the Commons, and he mentioned his grandfather's retirement party. Then, he asked if I would go with him.

I'm not sure if it's because he didn't want to make the drive alone or because we haven't left each other's sight since the night we first had sex. Or maybe it's because, now that I'm here and seeing his family, I realize these people are sharks out for blood. Yeah, I wouldn't want to attend this thing solo either.

"Good to see you, too. Happy retirement." Austin hands his grandfather a long-shaped gift bag in hunter green, and I know that there is a priceless scotch in there because he told me on the ride up.

"And you brought a date. To your grandfather's party. Trying to upstage me?" His grandfather lifts a judgmental, bushy white eyebrow.

I feel my insides cower but paste an innocent smile on my face and extend my hand. "Mr. Van Hewitt, congratulations on all of your hard work. My name is Taya, I actually grew up in Webton. What you've done in this town and for it is a great accomplishment."

The elder head of the family puffs out his chest at the compliment. "Well, thank you. Even if he did bring an uninvited guest, my grandson sure does know how to pick them pretty."

God, *gross*. Austin reaches for my hand, laces his fingers through mine, and squeezes. Kind of as if he's saying, *I'm sorry about this, but thank you for being here*. The secret form of body language meant only for me makes my heart skip a beat.

"We're going to go say hi to the family." Austin gives him a tight smile and leads me away by the hand.

But instead of going to see his family or be introduced to his parents, he pulls me into the hallway of the restaurant where his grandfather's party is taking place. Gino's, a local Italian catering company, is known for its penne vodka and cannolis. I've been here a number of times for various events but in a room full of Van Hewitt's, I don't feel much like chowing down or dancing. Not that they're playing music that's fit for anything but a funeral.

Austin pulls me in, his lips pressed against my temple, as he hugs me like I might be some escape from these people. "I should not have brought you here. These people are horrible."

I chuckle into his chest, breathing in the scent of sage and cedar. "At least I have no desire to become a Van Hewitt now."

He pulls back, assessing my expression, and then throws his head back and laughs. "Now, of all times, you decide to not only make fun of yourself but also my family and their ego? I mean, are you not perfect?"

The way my soul rises out of my body's, dies, and goes to heaven at him thinking I'm perfect ... the boob sweat is *real*. Although, anytime he looks at me nowadays, I start sweating. Because it's either one of two ways, with a smile on his face because of something I've said or with desire so strong it nearly bowls me over.

I guess you could say we've been *seeing* each other? I'm not sure if that's the right word, but for the last five days, things have kind of just fallen into place without us having a conversation about it. Since I woke up in his bed Saturday morning, after the most earth-shattering sex I've ever had, we've been inseparable. He refused to let me leave his attic bedroom, instead making a very convincing argument as to why I should stay there all day when he moved down my body and put his mouth between my thighs.

We spent the morning in bed, which bled into the afternoon, and by the time Bevan found us while wondering if I was going to the house party down the street, it was nearly nine p.m. Needless to say, the girls are thrilled. When they found out, they texted me every other minute about the sex, what he's like, and everything in between.

I'm not one to kiss and tell, but I couldn't not fill my best friends in on the fact that Austin Van Hewitt is, in fact, a sex god. Holy smokes, the guy is ... I don't know. Legendary? That seems a ridiculous word to use, but it's the only one that comes to mind.

The sex. My god, *the sex*. I have to press the backs of my hands to my reddening cheeks in the middle of this retirement party just thinking about it. Austin is intense. Demanding. *Dirty*. I was not expecting that from the guy who washes his dishes immediately after eating off of them. I knew he was a good kisser, but Jesus Christ, I've never had better, more mind-blowing, more orgasmic sex. Obviously, my experience is limited, and he's two years older. But he's the type of guy I will compare everyone else to going forward.

Not that I hope I have to. I'm aware we've only been good and solid for four days, but those four days have felt better than any in my life. Which is why it's not too strange that he asked me to come with him today, especially since I'm from his hometown.

I shrug, flipping my hair. "I guess I really am."

"If only we could just drive back to school and forget all of these bastards." Austin rests his forehead on mine.

"Can't we?" I suggest, very much wanting to be in his bed right now.

"Not if I don't want to hear about it for the next twenty years." He rolls his eyes. "We should get back in there. I have to make appropriate appearance time or my dad will bring the thunder."

He straightens, rolls his shoulders, and I see the Van Hewitt mask slide into place. I can't believe I haven't realized it all these years. He's not the Austin I truly know and want to be with when he's in this mode of carrying his family's last name.

We make our way around the room, fielding questions from his relatives ranging from snarky to downright rude. The whole lot of Van Hewitts is just competing against each other at what should be a laid-back family party. I know my brood has issues, but Christmas isn't a volleyball match of conversation to see who dropped the most money on a car this year or who opened more businesses.

Austin hasn't let go of my hand, and I'm not sure if he's holding it because he wants to feel my fingers laced with his or because he needs an anchor in the middle of all these assholes.

"Son, nice to see you showed up, though you've avoided me

all night." I turn as Austin does and see Mr. Van Hewitt, his father, standing before us.

Of course, I've seen the guy around town, I've seen most of these people around town. Especially Austin's two cousins who were in my grade, Miley and Cassandra. Their jaws nearly hit the floor today when they saw me walking around with him. Those two were so snooty and popular growing up, simply because they had money. It wasn't like I, or Bevan, or Amelie, were lacking for attention in school. But we were second-tier popular, under the shiny stars of the kids who would peak after we all grew up and left our hometown.

But Austin's father, well, you'd have to live under a rock in Webton not to know him. He owns one of the biggest real estate firms in the area, is the top donor to the high school basketball teams, and is generally involved in any big construction project you hear about in town.

"Dad." Austin sticks out his hand and his father shakes it.

Then he leans into the woman standing next to his father, kisses her Botoxed and filled cheeks, then straightens. "Mom."

His parents look like they're attending a comedy show put on by the grim reaper. Either that or his mother is a walking poster child for how smiling gives you laugh lines.

"This is Taya North. She grew up here in Webton, and I'm currently subletting the room in her and her friends' house," he explains.

His father gives me a once-over, then dismisses me without a single word. The mother barely even lets her gaze wander over me.

"I want you to talk to Uncle Gene tonight about possibly coming in on the strip mall deal. They could use you on the project after graduation, but right now they're ramping up and—"

"Dad, we talked about me helping Aunt Miriam at the TV

network. I want to put my degree to good use." Clearly, by the tone of both their voices, this is a fight they've had many times.

As best as I can, I watch Austin in my peripheral. His face is stone, the frustrated clip to his voice betraying how he feels about his father's request. I know he's a radio major, obviously, but it never occurred to me that his family would try to stop him from going into that field. I guess this is what he means when he says the last name comes with strings.

Now that I think about it, I don't know a single Van Hewitt in Webton who works outside of the family businesses.

"And I told you, you had four years to play around with your little passion and then it was time to get to work." His father sneers at him.

"*Dad.*" The word is a barely hidden growl of a warning.

"Let's not do this here." His mother lays a hand on his father's arm. "We don't want the family getting any sense of tension, do we now?"

I want to roll my eyes at how *Stepford Wives* they're being but try to remain neutral. It's clear that I'm not the only person in this pairing with mommy/daddy issues.

"Your uncle is expecting your call. You need to respect that." His father's parting shot is a command.

Austin lets out an audible sigh, then turns to me. The Van Hewitt mask has fallen, and in those captivating eyes I see only the guy whose bed I've spent four days barely getting out of.

"Come on, let's sneak out."

"Won't you get in trouble? They haven't even cut that massive cake, which I'm sure none of your girl cousins will even eat." Such a shame, since the frosting looks three layers deep.

"Nah, no one will notice. I showed my face, they got their punches in, so we're golden." The way his sarcasm doesn't reach his eyes makes my heart hurt.

"Let's go then. You can blame it on me, one of Webton's flooziest."

Austin leans in close as we exit the catering hall, his lips tracing the outer shell of my ear. "Only for me."

There are a few main shopping areas or streets to be seen on in Webton, but none more than the Eastwick Mall. With its giant food court, floors and floors of stores, and warm place to adventure from the cold in the harsh Upstate New York winters, it's always been a hot spot in town. Starting from the age of twelve, many a weekend nights were spent here. The girls and I would roam around in search of other Webton pre-teens or teens to hang out with or boys to flirt with. Or we'd catch a movie in the theater attached to the mall, or see who could fit the most pretzel bites in their mouth, or challenge each other to walk up the down escalator.

My youth had been spent here, but we would definitely see people we knew. What would they say when they saw me with Austin? I am relatively unknown in this town, other than being the sister of that girl who was going to the Olympics.

"Why do we need to come here?" I hedge, anxious as we walk into the building.

Austin and I fall into step side by side, but he doesn't reach for my hand like he did at his grandfather's party. A sense of rejection nestles into my bones like an old, prickly friend.

"I just have to pick up this mic I put on hold at an electronics store, it's pretty rare, and I found it here. Sorry, we'll get going soon." He smiles down at me, and I get distracted by the sandy blond stubble on his chin.

"Well, I'll have to get a cinnamon pretzel now that we're

here. Seeing as you didn't let me stay for cake," I joke as we walk through the mall.

"Remember the milkshake stand that had those awesome peanut butter chocolate milkshakes? I miss that place." Austin references one of the most popular stands in the mall from our childhood.

Two girls from Austin's grade pass us, then do a double take. I see them before he does, but he clocks them when they start to whisper loudly about what "*that girl*," meaning me, is doing with Austin Van Hewitt.

That's when he seems to snap out of the haze he's been in since we left Gino's, and I feel his hand reach for mine. The moment our fingers lock, my whole body is at peace. My skin flushes, my heart begins to beat double time, the butterflies in my stomach take off in flight.

We grab Austin's microphone from an electronics store that has me scared to touch anything inside and then begin to make our way back to the car.

But as we walk into the department store we parked near, the pair walking toward us are two people I never expected to see on my short trip up here.

"Taya?"

My mother looks at me like she can't believe I'm really standing in front of her, and Kathleen looks back and forth between my companion and me.

"Oh, woah. Hi, Mom. Hi, Kath." I'm a little bit in shock, seeing them here when I wasn't going to even drop in to check up with my family.

We hug and kiss, and the actions feel forced. Austin stands where he is until I introduce him, and he gives my mother and sister friendly smiles.

"Nice to meet you," he says, holding my hand.

Kathleen won't stop staring at the place where we're joined.

"I didn't know you were coming into town," Mom says, smoothing her hair behind her ear.

She's flustered, and I'm not sure if it's because I caught her off guard or if it's because I'm the daughter she never really connects with.

"Austin had a thing, and he asked me to come with him. Didn't want to bother you guys if you had a training or practice or something."

I try to keep the bitterness out of my tone, but it still creeps in. Austin squeezes my hand, as if he can sense I'm in an awkward family conversation now. How does he know, this soon, just what I'm feeling?

"Oh my gosh, honey, you could have called us! We would have loved to see you." Mom laughs as if I'm making some sort of joke.

Meanwhile, they've barely called to check in since I got back to college in January.

"How is everything going, Kath?" I nod, asking the question out of politeness.

My sister blinks. "Good. I have a competition in London next week."

Nothing about her personal life or how she's actually *feeling*, just all about the horses. This is why we will never understand each other.

"Well, we have to get back to campus." I shuffle my feet.

Wouldn't it be wonderful to grab coffee and sit and chat? Austin and I are in no rush. Normally, a girl would be so excited to introduce a guy like Austin to her family. A normal family would joke and walk the mall shopping, maybe do a stupid little try-on like those montages in the movies.

But we're not most families. I feel disconnected, like an outsider to the people who are my blood. Now that I think about it, Austin and I have that in common.

"Okay. It was so good to see you, sweetheart. Let's chat this week, okay?" Mom gives me a bright smile.

Yeah, right. She's going to London with my sister, which means she'll forget she ever promised that.

This trip to Webton has shown me some new things about Austin, but it has also exposed sides of me that I don't know if I am ready to reveal to him.

As we get in the car, part of me wishes we could have just stayed in our Prospect Street bubble forever.

The first ten minutes of the car ride are quiet, the darkness shrouding us as David Bowie hums through the speakers.

It's nearly seven p.m., and we haven't hit daylight savings yet, so I can't make out Taya's expression, though I want to, terribly.

"Thank you for coming with me today."

I reach across the center console and put my hand on her knee, then squeeze. Though she has jeans on and I can't run my hand over her smooth skin, this is the most comforted I've felt all day. There is something about Taya that puts me at ease, almost like I can be my most authentic self when I'm around her. It might have been a last-minute invite, but I'm glad she's with me today. And there is something about her being in the room with my family that shows her something about me I could never explain.

Apparently, the universe is throwing us all kinds of demonstrations today, since we ran into her family at the mall. From the way she was with her mother and sister, it's clear that there is just as much tension in that relationship as the one I have with my parents.

When Taya doesn't answer, I realize she's so preoccupied that she didn't hear me.

"It was nice to meet your mom and sister," I toss it out, wondering what she'll say.

Because while it was nice to meet some of her family, the whole thing felt more awkward than my grandfather's entire party. Taya knows a lot about my family because of who they are in Webton, but I guess I never really realized hers has baggage too. It's a big flaw of mine, my inability to look past my own life's drama and issues. When I do, I realize that a lot of the people around me have shit going on too. In that regard, it makes me feel closer to this beautiful girl whose mind I suddenly want to pick apart.

"Yeah." She nods, clearly lost in her own head.

"Your sister is the Olympian, right?" I throw the question out, waiting to see when Taya will actually talk to me.

A quick glance away from the highway and in her direction shows me that she's deep in thought, staring out the passenger side window.

"Not yet, but yes, she's on her way." The sarcastic end note to her sentence alerts me that it's a sensitive topic.

But just like my family and me, you get to know people by the chatter in Webton. It's a big suburb with a small-town feel, and everyone is always in everyone else's business. And those people loved to know the business of Webton's most famous, or infamous, residents. I didn't put two and two together when I met her, or even when we saw her sister in the mall. But now that I think about it, I've heard things about her sister and those horse competitions. Taya's sister was going to be a local celebrity after her brush with the Olympics, so of course, some towns-people want to ride her coattails or be attached to her.

"Were you planning on seeing your family when we were in town?" Another question and I'm sure she'll try to dodge it.

Taya chuckles, but the tone is far from amusement or humor. "No. If I had, they probably wouldn't have even known I was there."

Well, that's a lot to unpack.

The headlights shine on the highway, and I move my hand up her thigh, searching for her hand. When I find it, I lace our fingers together. It's starting to get difficult whenever I have to let her go in any way. I crave holding her in whatever way I can and find myself reaching out subconsciously.

"What do you mean?" I don't want to push, but she seems to be letting a wall down, and I want to topple it.

She sighs but takes her other hand and begins rubbing her thumb on mine where our hands are joined. The motion relaxes me, and I wish like hell we were out of this car and in one of our beds.

"My mom hasn't called in weeks. She and my dad have barely been up to see me since I came to college. They're always jetting off to Kathleen's competitions, though it's been that way since we were kids, so I don't know why I expect anything more. When I am home, the conversation always turns to horses, or equipment, or whatever the fuck they're doing for Kathleen next. So I really don't go. I don't know, it's been like this most of my life. I feel like they barely know me, and my mom, as you can see, has no idea how to talk to me. As if it's that hard. Kathleen is the abnormal child, by all standards."

Her voice nearly breaks, but she covers it up, and by the way she physically shrugs, I can tell she's been burying these emotions for as long as her sister has been riding horses.

"I'm sorry, Taya." I say it simply because no amount of me trying to fix anything will help.

Sometimes, things just suck, and that's all.

"It's nothing, really." She looks away again.

The highway stretches in front of us, and I wish so badly I

could pull over and kiss her right now, but I want to get us home and upstairs so we can do way more than kiss.

My hand squeezes in hers. "No, it is something. You saw how messed up my family is. I know how that kind of tension takes a toll. It's pretty unfair that your mom and dad dedicate so much time to your sister, but can't seem to make a few minutes to call you."

The shaky breath she takes is laced with tears. "That's just the tip of the iceberg. I mean, you name a big moment in my life, and I guarantee one of my parents missed it because they were off at a competition with Kathleen. Eighth grade graduation, my first varsity basketball game, the time I got inducted into French honor society, even prom. Only my dad could drop me off at college because Kath was competing in equestrian nationals in Georgia. I just feel forgotten."

God, the despair in her voice absolutely guts me. I hate that she feels so unseen, that I contributed to that not so long ago. This girl is brilliant, gorgeous, and so humble and laid-back that it makes me want to spend every moment with her.

"I see you. I will never forget you." Removing my hand from hers, I run the back of it over her cheek, caressing that velvety smooth skin. She closes her eyes, leaning into my touch, and I feel it.

The healing we're providing each other. Her, by coming with me into the den of lions that is my family. She stood tall and didn't need any special consideration. Taya simply supported me and was the steady presence she always is. Swimming with the sharks usually makes my blood boil, but I find myself pretty calm on this drive home. That's because of her.

And I hope I can give her the same. She deserves to be seen on every level; she deserves to be the priority and have her accomplishments celebrated. It's been mere days since we became attached at the hip, but I feel like I know her on a level deeper than almost anyone I've encountered thus far.

Maybe it's because we are both broken in the same way and just want someone to see the real person underneath.

"I think I'm going to throw up."

Amelie leans on me, her head on my shoulder, as I drape my legs across Bevan's lap. We've always watched TV like this since we were kids, all over each other. Bevan usually scratches my arm with her blood red, coffin-shaped nails, and I'm in heaven. Is there a better feeling than someone softly tickling your arm or back? Sex be damned.

"You're not. He's a douchebag. Just think of him as a douchebag." Bevan flicks off Gannon's face on the TV screen.

I'm not sure why we're watching this or why we agreed to let Amelie watch the entire season of the reality dating show Gannon left college to go on. They started filming weeks ago and still are, since we can't reach him by phone or email thanks to production's rules. But they're now airing the first episodes, and it's *brutal* on Amelie.

So we decided we're all going to watch together. That means viewing a shitty reality show on a Thursday night when we could be out, or I could be up in Austin's bedroom. Which is where I'd rather be, no offense to my best friends, but I've had

years with them. Austin and I are just discovering our groove ...
and his moves. Wink face. I could discover that guy *all* day long.

But Amelie is so shook by this. Imagine being the girl who
has been head over heels in love with her best friend, who leads
her on in terrible fashion, for more than half her life. Then
imagine that said love of her life decides to date a woman on TV,
professing his attraction to her every other scene when he
barely knows the girl.

On the screen, Gannon is blathering on about falling for
some girl who looks like a Kardashian-replica Instagram model.
She's draped all over his lap in a bikini bottom that can only be
classified as dental floss, and I'm pretty sure he's three shots in.

Then he drops *the* line.

"I think I'm falling in love with you. I could spend my life
with you," says an on-screen Gannon, and then the upcoming
scenes after the commercials flash to him looking at diamond
rings.

Bevan actually sits up and sprays the drink of soda she just
took all over the room. "I'm sorry, *what the fuck did he just say*?"

My ears are ringing, and I have to shake off my shirt sleeve
from where she just soaked it in Diet Coke.

"He's thinking about proposing to her! Proposing? He's
twenty fucking years old. What's he going to say next? 'I could
see myself marrying her.' Is he fucking serious?"

Tears stream down her face, and I can honestly hear the
cracks fracturing her heart right now. Bevan and I exchange a
look, knowing we should put a stop to watching this. But at the
same time are completely aware that Amelie will just go to her
bedroom and watch endless clips of this on YouTube.

"Come here." I pull her into a hug, and she begins to sob into
my sweatshirt.

I have to hand it to Gannon, though. The guy is good. He's
going to get his fifteen minutes and more, which is what he's

always wanted. Gannon is the flashy star that was way too big for Webton even when we were eight. He was voted "most likely to be famous" in our senior year yearbook. The guy is charming, gorgeous, has this wicked little smile, and knows exactly how to turn on his best self for a camera.

Yeah, I have no doubt he'll be the darling of this franchise in no time. Meanwhile, I'm going to have to pick my best friend up off the floor each day for years to come. So, I fucking hate the guy right now.

"*Aimer, ce n'est pas se regarder l'un l'autre, c'est regarder ensemble dans la même direction*," I tell her, enunciating each word.

"When you speak French, it helps a little." She wipes a tear from her cheek. "What does it mean?"

"Antoine de St-Exupéry wrote it. It means 'Love doesn't mean gazing at each other, but looking, together, in the same direction.' I think it fits with you. You're only gazing at Gannon, blinded by the man you want to see. But he isn't looking in the same direction. He's not even looking, he's got his head buried so far up his own ass—"

"We get it, you poet." Bevan chuckles. "But she is right, Am, no matter how harsh it sounds. You deserve someone who looks in the same direction with you, *at you*. Believe me, I know how fucked up love is. But you, out of all of us, deserve happiness. Gannon is a pig. Let's leave him in the shit and move on."

Amelie seems to be digesting the truth, and I hate having to be so direct, but she needs to hear this.

"But look at Taya. She got her happy ending." She points to me.

"First of all, I've been seeing Austin on consistent, good terms for like a week. I wouldn't call that a happy ending." But in my heart, I know how happy I am and how much I'm counting on this to last.

"Exactly," Bevan says. "Plus, remember that movie? *He's Just*

Not That Into You? Taya is the exception, not the rule. And she may become the rule. Hell, she was the rule for like a billion years before he even noticed her."

"Thanks, Bev." I roll my eyes, a little hurt at her insinuation that Austin and I are just a fling.

"You know what I'm trying to say. This is about Amelie."

I love Bevan to my core, but sometimes her dismissiveness can cut deep. I try to focus on our friend though, and what we're trying to get across to her.

"All I'm saying," Bevan continues, "is maybe it's time to get on some dating apps. At least talk to another guy. Text flirt. It'll improve your mood."

Amelie looks back at the TV, where Gannon's face appears again. "Maybe you're right. Maybe it's time to move on and look for someone who actually wants to be with me."

There is a note of hope in her voice, so I'll take it. But as we settle back into our typical positions to watch the rest of the show, I can't help but think about what Bevan said and that I was nearly in Amelie's position just weeks ago.

I can't forget that. For as much as I'm living in the honeymoon period of hooking up with Austin and hoping for a lot more than that, I can't let myself get carried away. The trip to Webton was a decent turning point, and I think we saw a side of each other that neither of us previously knew. But I got swept up in his aura before, before I even really knew him, and I have to put that age-old crush in the back of my mind.

Because Bevan could be right. This could dissolve between us because of either party. And while that makes my heart ache, I can't put all of my eggs in one basket.

I'll end up like Amelie, sobbing over a boy who will never feel the same way about me.

Reaching toward my bedside drawer, I grab a condom and roll it on.

"Ride me," I growl at Taya, flopping onto my back and putting my hands behind my head.

Hazel eyes, swirled with aquamarine and mocha, flash with lust. She takes in my naked body, all of her slim curves prowling over me like some kind of panther. Christ, how I worship this woman. She's flushed, and a little sheen of sweat glistens on her. I've had her on her back, my mouth between her legs, for the last ten minutes and she's already come once. The taste of her remains on my tongue, and watching her mount me and take my cock in her hand to slide down onto is like my holy grail.

"You feel so fucking good." She runs her hands through her hair, and I will keep this mental picture in my memory forever.

In no time, the way she's bouncing up and down on my cock has me nearly coming. "Slow down, babe."

The nickname just slips out, and it's odd because I typically don't use it. But with her, it fits.

"*Lo desideravo da molto tempo.*"

Taya's words curl into my ear like the most seductive drug. "What does it mean?"

I don't even know what language she's speaking, but I want more of it. Every time she whispers those accented words, my cock twitches inside her.

"Now, why would I tell you that?" Her voice is breathy and husky.

Without warning, I flip her, pinning her hands against the bed, and grind into her in long, fluid strokes. "Because if you don't, I'll torture you. I'll go just the right pace to make it feel incredible, but not deep or fast enough to give you that orgasm you're trembling for."

Another girl would lie back, beg me, or just tell me what she'd said. Not Taya. Instead, she pulls her hands free of mine and rakes her nails down my back just a little too hard, so the pain morphs into pleasure. Then she bites her lip, licking it after releasing it, and her teeth marks are still on her skin.

"You do not play fair." I growl, because with every little seduction, I'm pumping harder.

I can't help it. This girl drives me insane. With every thrust, her hips come up to meet me. My balls slap on her ass. Her eyes begin to roll back, and I can feel the sensation of my climax tingle at the base of my spine.

"Come. Now," I command her, pistoning my hips as fast as I can.

My cock is so deep inside of her when she explodes that all of her muscles grip my dick like a fist. I come, shouting my release, and nearly blackout from the intensity.

I can barely feel my body and feel it all too much at the same time. Beneath me, Taya is still mewling from her release.

Once we've caught our breath, I start tracing her spine with the tip of my fingers. Outside, someone shouts on the street, and birds are chirping. The sunlight shines through onto the carpet, and Taya groans.

"I have class," she whines but doesn't move from where my hand is slowly stroking her back.

"Skip it." It's an automatic response. "We'll make this afternoon quickie a true afternoon delight."

She chuckles into my chest, then looks up at me with a sarcastic expression. "Some of us aren't seniors and have to go to class. Plus, I love my courses. Where else am I going to speak different languages where people actually understand me?"

"You just love that you can say things and I have no idea what they mean, don't you?" I swat her butt.

"Kind of." She shrugs, a sheepish little smile sneaking over her lips. "I mean, let's be real, you know so much of my inner thoughts from that letter that it feels nice to have an outlet where you have no idea what I'm feeling."

It's easier for her to address the time capsule letter now, but I still sense the tension between us when it comes to that.

"What is it that drew you to me? I mean, I was a dumbass teenager who cared more about basketball and playing video games than I did about girls."

"Oh, come on, Austin. You can't tell me you aren't aware of how you came off in high school. You were the most popular kid in school, not to mention our town. You won homecoming king all four years. And I mean ... look at you."

She waves her hand up and down my naked body, the one she just rode like she was a professional cowgirl.

"Well, it's yours to explore now if you want to." I stretch out, the cockiness in my voice shining through.

She takes one of my pillows and cowers under it; her voice muffled as she says, "All right, can we stop the 'embarrass Taya time' now? Please?"

I pull her in, shimmying down the bed to press kisses into

her stomach. "Well, beautiful, I have some affection to make up for."

"And I," she rolls out of my grip, "need to go to class. I'll leave you here to think about all the ways you can make it up to me."

"What an interesting idea." I flop back, tapping my finger to my chin.

As Taya pulls the black lacy boy shorts over her hips, a sight that makes my dick hard but also makes me want to slide them off all over again, she tries to ask me what she assumes is a simple question.

"So, big bad senior, what will it be after graduation? A job in radio, I'm assuming."

Of all the things we've talked about in the last week or so, this isn't one of them. Maybe we're both avoiding the fact that I'll be leaving here in May. Maybe I just haven't wanted to address it because I still have no idea what the hell I'm going to do.

"Maybe … it's complicated." I try not to get too in-depth.

"Ah, I remember your dad basically threatening you into that job with your uncle." She comes back over to sit on the bed as she clasps her bra and pulls her T-shirt over her head.

"Yeah, that kind of complicated." I can tell Taya wants me to spill a little more, so I sigh and try to articulate. "I want to be in sports radio. More than anything. I've actually been applying to stations all over the country and have an interview for a lowly assistant to one of the on-air talents at a station in New York City. But it would be a foot in the door."

She takes my face in her hands; her smile all excitement. "Austin! That's amazing!"

I shake my head humbly and turn my lips to kiss one of her palms. "Yeah, yeah. I mean, it's just an interview. But if my dad ever found out I was looking outside of the family business, he'd come down here and kill me with his bare hands. I'm a Van Hewitt, I don't get a choice. Going into the family business is what everyone before me has done, and what everyone will continue to do. Moving back to Webton is a non-negotiable to him, and I know if I do that, I'll be miserable."

She frowns, her eyebrows drawing in. "Then what is there to think about? Your happiness comes first. Always. Why go live a life you don't even want?"

"Because my family would turn against me. Most of them would never talk to me again. I'd be the black sheep, cast out. And yeah, I don't have a supportive family to begin with, and most of them are absolute sharks out for blood. But there is a big difference between having a crappy family and not having one at all. I'm not sure I'm ready to find out what it's like being all alone in this world."

Taya nods, her expression growing sad. She can grasp that, because while we might not love the situations we're both in with our respective families, considering not having them at all is a scary thought.

"Well, I think you're going to kill that interview. And with how dedicated you are to the radio station, you'd be brilliant in New York City. I think you could really be something, Austin."

Taya has started to listen to my show with Gio. And although she says she couldn't care less about the sports talk, she told me that my voice coming through her car speakers gets her hot. Which, in turn, gets me hot. I can barely sit in the booth anymore without thinking about her circling her clit to my voice in her car. The thought has my dick twitching even now.

"Thanks." My head takes over, realizing how she's just complimented me.

There aren't many people around me who support what I actually want to do with my life. And here she is, doing it without question.

A sense that something bigger is happening between us hangs in the air as Taya leans in to give me one last kiss before heading downstairs and out the door to class. I pull her in, taking the kiss deeper, and lean into the feeling.

Maybe it wouldn't be such a bad thing to chase the high she provides. Maybe I've been waiting for her. Maybe it could work when I leave Talcott.

The spark of hope inside me is both dangerous and thrilling. And I'm too infatuated with Taya to blow it out.

L avender fills my nostrils, along with sage and a hint of lemon.

I put the soap down, trying not to gag, and smile at the small business owner. She's looking at me like I'm going to purchase one of her organic soaps, but they smell more like cleaning products than something I want lingering on my skin.

Walking along the row after I exit her stall, I link up with Bevan and Amelie as we peruse the farmer's market.

This collection of local good's sellers, which is about a fifteen-minute drive from our house in the opposite direction of campus, overlooks the lake. The outdoor, open-air market is comprised of a wooden structure with dozens of different stalls for different businesses selling their goods. There are candle makers, vegetable farmers, CBD producers, and all kinds of organic or natural products. The college town around Talcott is known for its hippie attitude, and so it's not uncommon to see people walking around downtown without shoes on or frequenting the shores of the lake completely naked. These are granola kind of people, and I kind of love it. I'm not ever going to be a vegan or wash my hair with shampoo made of sap and beeswax, but I can appreciate how they're trying to make the planet a better place.

I can also appreciate their delicious assortment of cheeses from a local dairy farm. I pop a piece of cheddar in my mouth and peruse the gouda they're displaying in their stall.

"We could get that with a fig jam and bake it," Bevan suggests, catching where my gaze is landing.

"It's not a bad idea. Would Callum eat it?" I question.

We're having a family dinner tonight. Well, of sorts. My roommates and I are actually having a *Top Chef* sort of challenge, boys vs. girls. We're both cooking an appetizer and a main course. Dessert is being provided via the famous macaroons they sell here at the farmer's market, because none of us are daring enough to be the pastry chef.

"Callum would eat Tide Pods if I put them in a bowl for him. He's that amenable."

"Please don't tell us you're trying to poison your boyfriend." Amelie cringes.

"Some days I'd like to," Bevan mutters, and I know they're on the rocks again.

I've been spending a lot of time with Austin, but I can still recognize when Bevan and Callum are in a spat. They've been avoiding each other, and I can feel another breakup coming, but don't want to upset her even more.

So I steer the conversation to our meal. "Okay, so we'll do a baked brie, fig jam, apple tart kind of thing for our appetizer. And then for the main course, I thought we could make a seafood lasagna. I found a fresh pasta stand, and that guy over there has really delicious looking fish. It's a bit different, but I think we could kill it. Yeah?"

Since I'm the one who can actually decently cook out of the three of us, my best friends just nod and follow my lead. We're walking through the market, which is packed on a Saturday afternoon, and I see a familiar sandy blond scalp towering over the crowd.

"We're going to beat you." Amelie sticks out her tongue at Austin as he approaches.

I swear, every time I see this man, he steals my breath. He's just too damn gorgeous for human consumption, and I have to take him in in pieces.

But before I can digest the whole picture of the demi-god before me, he swoops in and plants a kiss on my lips. In public, in front of my friends. We haven't had the exclusive talk, but I feel like it's unneeded. Where the hell else would this boy be the six hours of the week we're not in each other's beds, having sex?

"Isn't this fraternizing with the enemy?" I smirk but wrap the arm not holding my basket of food items around his waist.

"I called a timeout. It was needed. I think, also, that we need to place a bet on tonight's competition." Austin leans in, whispering in my ear, "Loser has to undress the winner with their teeth."

"And that's a punishment how?" I grin, everything south of my waist tingling.

When I look around, I see Bevan and Amelie have ditched us, and so Austin and I start to explore by ourselves. Technically, we're supposed to be with our teams, but it's all for fun, and I have the most fun when I'm with him.

I glance up at him, and his brows are furrowed.

"You seem preoccupied." Not just today, but this week.

We walk side by side, ducking into the odd stall, looking at necklaces or investigating shampoos made from hemp oil.

"I had my interview for that position in New York. It was yesterday." He doesn't elaborate.

"You didn't say." I put it simply, knowing he doesn't want me to bounce up and down like an excited puppy.

I've learned, over the past weeks, that Austin is in deep with this huge mental dilemma about what to do when it comes to his future. I try to just listen, because he seems so conflicted about what to do.

"It went pretty well. They seemed impressed that I ran the station here. And I gave them good examples of my all-time favorite broadcasters. But part of me can't help but hope I *don't* get it."

"So you don't have to explain it to your family." I nod, knowing where this is headed.

"Every time I think about telling them, I freak out in my own head." He shakes it as if the panic is already starting up there. "At the same time, I can't imagine going back to Webton. That's the God's honest truth. I hate it there."

I'm not a huge fan of our hometown, and I probably wasn't going to live there after college, but his disdain is on another level.

"Why, though? I mean, I know more about you now. About your family. But compared to a lot of other people, you had it good. Money, popularity, anything you could want. Yes, you have to put up with their bullshit, but you have something waiting for you. People who actually want you around, who want you to stand for them and for the family."

I could understand his hesitancy, especially if they wouldn't let him go into radio. But part of me would kill for a family who had expectations of me. Who wanted me to come back and carry their legacy. To my parents and sister, I'm a nobody. Nothing is expected of me, and no one really cares if I hang around. In a way, I crave the pressure Austin has.

"Everywhere I went, every time someone talked to me, it was always about my last name. What mystery it carried, what I could give them. I was so sick of the attention that I wanted to hide under a rock and never come out. I can't imagine ever embracing that. I can't imagine living that day in and day out, and having to compete with my family to do so. I don't want some wife who only craves the Van Hewitt name, I can't imagine bragging about my kids like a snob at the same soccer games my dad bragged about me at."

I shrug and give him a small smile. "I get it. I do. But, it's clear that you've never experienced the reverse of that."

I don't mean to make it about me, but Austin doesn't quite see that the problems he has? They're not really problems.

He inches closer to me. "That's why you hide yourself? Why you're okay in the background?"

Damn, how did he realize I do that? I'm not one to call attention to myself, and I generally hang back in the thick of a crowd. But I always thought I was decent at blending in. Apparently, to the right person, everything you do will be noticed.

"I didn't think anyone noticed that." I cast my eyes down.

"Fuck, I feel like such a prick. How did I ever overlook you?" His words are hushed, and there he goes again, stealing my breath. "I notice everything you do. Well, now. I notice now. I'm sorry, Taya. I'm sorry I was a selfish high school kid in my own head. I can't believe I ever passed up the chance ..."

The desperation to make me understand is apparent in his voice, and I see it. I do. I don't blame him for anything, not anymore. The letter scandal seems years behind us.

"You get pretty good at being invisible when no one wants to see you. I spent years sitting on a bench, watching my parents pour all of their love and energy into my sister. I'm good at blending into the background. But it's nice to be seen."

My cheeks heat, and I have to say the next words, even if they're a little cheesy and embarrassing. But I don't want to hold anything back from him.

"The only person I want to be seen by is you. When you look at me, it's like ..." I break off, too overwhelmed to put the feeling into words.

Austin reaches for me and presses his forehead to mine. "I know. I know. Sometimes I feel like I'm going crazy."

He's not really saying anything, and neither am I. Yet, we understand each other on a cellular level. Maybe I knew how strong our connection would be all the way back when I wrote that time capsule letter. There is this *click* in me whenever I see him or when I saw him back then. I kind of just *knew*. And now that we're actually together, it does feel crazy how *big* this whole thing feels.

"This is a bit intense for the farmer's market, isn't it?" I chuckle but don't move.

Neither does he, and we're standing at the exit to the wooden pavilion, Cayuga Lake sparkling in the distance. The rolling hills melt down to the crystalline water, and it goes for miles, until you can only see waves and horizon.

"You know I'm going to kick your culinary ass, right?" As Austin says it, he lightly smacks my butt.

His aim has the desired effect, sending tingles through my core, and I have to hide the shiver running up my spine in the name of competitive game face.

"We'll see about that. I think you might be the one undressing me with your teeth." Pushing away, I swing my hips and look back at him as I walk off.

"In that case, I'm throwing the competition," he yells after me.

I tip my head back and laugh, marveling at how good my life is right now.

"Is that fire?"

Bevan points to one of the boy's burners, and sure enough, boiling water is pouring out of the stove and onto the kitchen floor.

"Oh, fuck!" Callum runs to the stove and flicks off the gas, fanning the boiling pot with his hands.

"Yeah, *that'll* work." I hear Austin chuckle from where he's chopping carrots at the cutting board.

"Do they get points deducted for almost burning down the house?" Amelie taps her chin.

"This isn't a gymnastics meet, Ams." Scott laughs, not helping in the slightest.

Austin is really the one running the show on the boys' side, which is definitely a turn-on. They're planning to make parmesan chicken wings as their appetizer, which is such a guy food. But Austin is attempting to make duck tacos for their main course, and I have to say, it smells fucking delicious. That is, if Callum doesn't burn the pot boiling water for their Cajun mashed potatoes that are going on the side.

The whole atmosphere in our house is giddy, everyone is

into the competition, and there is no drama going on between us roommates at the moment. It's one of those peaceful times where all I can think is, *life is good.*

I'm chopping the apples for our brie bake when I hear him.

"Blame it all on my roots!"

Austin's random outburst of song has us all turning to face him, and Scott just starts laughing. It's so out of character for my guy, the call for attention whether he realizes it as that or not. Austin is usually pretty quiet and lets his looks or aura do the talking. People are naturally drawn to him, and I've learned he's actually pretty shy and reserved.

But him busting out in a Garth Brooks' tune is shocking and also pretty damn sexy.

"I showed up in boots!" Amelie continues, smiling at the guy who has captured my heart.

It's one thing to be falling in love with a guy. It's another thing entirely when your friends also accept him and bring them into their inner circle. That's what tonight feels like, and the smile on my face is so wide it starts to hurt my cheeks.

"And ruined your black-tie affair," Scott, Callum, and Austin all sing together.

There is also something downright hot about three hulking males cooking and singing an old country tune. Completely domestic, effortlessly handsome, and I get a front row seat.

"The last one to know, the last one to show, I was the last one you thought you'd see there!" I contribute, my pipes a little rusty.

We all join in, besides Bevan, who hates country music, and start to belt out the lyrics. Everyone is shaking their hips, walking around the kitchen checking on our dishes, and the whole atmosphere makes me want to weep. It's one of those special moments that I want to soak in, because I know it will be a golden memory when I play it back in my head years from now.

When it gets to the chorus, I wrap an arm around Bevan's neck and shake her until she sings.

"'Cause I've got friends in *low* places, where the whiskey drowns and the beer chases my blues away," I sing in her ear, and she finally rolls her eyes and jumps in.

Scott grabs a bottle of whiskey from the counter and begins to pour shots.

The whole thing is comical and perfect in the best way possible, and our little family sing-a-long is a scene out of a movie. These are the moments in life that I wish I could capture on a loop and carry with me in my back pocket.

In the end, the girls win the cooking competition, though the whole meal is delicious. And I win the best prize of all, because Austin is waiting for me in bed after I washed my face and took the day off.

Oh, and he was completely naked.

Gio, Brian, and Evan's living room is so dirty, I can barely find an open space to sit on the couch.

"You guys are gross," I complain, so happy I decided not to live here.

There's something to be said about living in a house that's half made up of women because a certain standard existed.

Brian shrugs. "No one who comes over seems to mind."

"Oh, believe me, they mind. They just see a football player and don't say anything." The girls who come around Brian are usually jersey groupies looking for one thing.

"Yo, Vanny!" Gio daps me up, walking into their living room and plopping down.

I've missed these guys since I've been spending so much time at my own house.

Another week has passed, and Taya and I have been together for about a month or so. We haven't had the conversation about whether or not we're exclusive, about whether or not she is my girlfriend and I am her boyfriend. It seems dumb, honestly, like we're in middle school or something. I think she's smart enough to know that I'm not interested or sleeping with anyone else, and I know the same when it comes to her.

Plus, I wouldn't say I'm avoiding having a conversation about being a couple, but I'm glad Taya isn't pushing it. With each passing day, and as the clock winds down to graduation, my anxiety ramps up. I have no idea what decisions I'm going to make, nor do I have a plan on how to decide. I feel like, when it comes to my career and future and relationship, I'm going to spin around at the last second with my eyes closed and see where my finger lands. Which is a horrible plan, but I can't bring myself to disappoint whole groups of people. It's the way I'm conditioned and have been since my father sunk his claws into me at birth.

"Haven't seen you around, dude." Evan is playing FIFA on the couch and barely waves.

"I know, sorry, guys. I, uh, haven't been down to the bars lately." I scratch the back of my neck.

"Because he's too busy getting pussy in his own damn house." Brian snorts, winking at me.

"Hey, hey, don't say it that way." Taya is so much more than pussy. Just saying the word like she's some hot hook up, which she was, degrades what we have.

"Sorry, sorry." He lifts his hands like a white flag.

"Yeah, that's his girl," Gio says, popping some chips in his mouth.

"You? A girlfriend? I'm kind of shocked." Brian looks like he might pick up a pile of random trash but then sits back down.

I don't correct him on the term girlfriend, because I kind of like how it sounds.

"Well, it was actually a non-starter for a little while there," I hedge, knowing I haven't really explained this to the guys yet.

"What do you mean?" Evan doesn't look up from the TV, but I know he's listening.

I haven't told anyone this up until now, and it feels like I'm gossiping about Taya or something. But these are my friends, and with the thoughts I've had recently, I need an outside opinion. Maybe they'll just think it's a funny story.

"I've told you guys about what my family is like ... like, who they are in my hometown?"

"The rich fucks who own everything? Yeah, you've told us." Brian snorts.

I chuck an empty beer can at him, but he ducks it. "Essentially, yes. By a completely freak accident of events, I got this letter at my college house. It wasn't addressed to anyone, but came from my freshman year English teacher from high school. So I opened it—"

"Was this teacher a hot chick? Was it full of nudes?" Evan again, still not making eye contact.

I roll mine. "The teacher was a dude, and this is not that kind of story. Also, who sends nudes in the mail anymore?"

Brian chuckles. "He has a point, Ev."

Gio jiggles his cell phone in the air. "All the nudes I need are on here."

"Yeah, your own." I laugh. "*Anyway*, I opened it, and it ended up not being mine. It was actually Taya's, but I didn't realize it until the end. I read the thing, and she ... uh, well, she gushes about me."

"In the letter?" Brian looks confused. "But how?"

"Well, I guess she's always had a crush on me, but I didn't realize that. Then I got that letter—"

"And you invaded her privacy and read it." That one's Evan, who still hasn't looked at me instead of the TV.

My gut clenches. "Yeah, I know I did."

"Dude, that's kind of *weird*." Gio eyes me, cocking his head to the side. "She was like, obsessed with you?"

"She really manifested that shit, huh?" Brian chimes in.

"It's like if you were a famous person or something. Some girl had your posters in her bedroom, and now you're dating her. It's like ... what's that movie? *Single White Female*?"

Evan doesn't understand that in Webton, I kind of *am* famous. That's not cocky, it's just stating a fact.

"No, none of that." I buzz their words away like they're annoying gnats. "I mean, I was freaked out about it. But now I'm not. I'm sure we all had embarrassing crushes when we were freshman."

"Yeah, I was into Demi Lovato. But I'm not currently pursuing her," Gio hedges.

"I'd just be careful, man." Evan finally sets his controller down. "With a girl like that, there will be a ton of expectations. She might not be voicing them now, but she's thought about this for a long time. You've been telling us that a commitment is the last thing you want. Actually, you've always said that. This girl? She's a whole-ass commitment."

My heart stammers in my chest, as if it's trying to defend what Taya and I have but can't form the words. They just don't get it; they don't know how we've passed it, and how much I've discovered about her when I really got to know her.

Brian whistles low. "Damn, since when did you go all *therapist* on us?"

Gio shrugs. "Ev kind of has a point, though. There is always something left to be desired when you think you're more into the person than they are into you. It gives the whole thing ... excitement, I guess. With that letter, you know all of her cards. And when you can't play the hand she wants dealt, what's going to happen?"

"So I should want someone who isn't as into me?" I chuckle, but it has a bitter tone to it.

"Not what I'm saying. Hey, man, you're the one who brought this up." Gio backs off, both verbally and physically.

He walks across the room, and part of me wonders why I told them in the first place. Gio's statement is ignorant. I've never wanted a girl who plays games, even if my friends do.

But in the back of my mind, haven't I thought some of the same things? Spending so much time with her has made me see just how unique and special of a person she is. There is still that pressure, though, the one I feel I need to measure up to to be the guy she wrote about in that letter. And my own insecurities about my hometown and who my family is ... that's not easily quieted.

I'm leaving Talcott University in just over a month. And then we'll be hours away, for years to come, if we decide to stay together.

The thought of Taya with someone else makes me want to punch one of the nasty walls in this house. But thinking about her comparing me to that fantasy guy when I can't be here for her?

I'm beginning to think that might be worse.

"Do we really need this many pillows in the bed?"

I pull one out from where it's wedged under my back. "Jeez, let's go up to my room and sleep there."

The woman sleeps with a zillion pillows, so many that there is barely room for the two of us on the mattress.

Taya hugs one to her naked chest. "They make me feel super comfy. Less lonely."

Beautiful, bare, and makeup free, she straddles my waist and hits me gently in the cheek with a pillow.

I flip her over, and she squeals. My teeth nip over her earlobe, and I whisper, "You don't ever need to feel lonely in this bed again. I'm here."

I'm not sure what I'm doing or where this is going. After my talk with my friends yesterday, Gio and I went to the radio station to do our show. I was distracted the entire time, called the wrong score of the tennis match, and flubbed a few other things. I was off my game, and my radio partner seemed judgmental. As if our conversation at his house, and my love life, contributed to it. Which in turn, made me panic, because if I was freaking out while doing my job at my college radio station, what would I be doing in my professional career if Taya and I stay together.

I'm not sure where I'll be in a month, but I won't be at Talcott. I swore up and down that during senior year, I wasn't getting into anything. I don't want a long-distance relationship, and if New York City works out, I'll have to focus all of my energy on busting my ass just to live because my family will cut me off.

Everything I've ever told myself I don't want, that's what Taya is. Younger, from my hometown, will have to stay at college when I leave, knows exactly who my family is, and what my last name means. The letter she wrote in freshman English should have been the biggest turnoff, but it's like we breezed right past it.

Because ... she's *her*. There is something that draws me to her subconsciously; I don't even know I'm leaning in or kissing her or walking to pick her up from whatever building she just had class in until I'm actually doing it.

My friend's words echo in my head, but I push them away. It's just another Thursday night, camped out in her room after our first round of sex. I'll probably wander downstairs for a snack, we'll fuck some more, and then I'll fall asleep with her in my arms. It's been our routine for weeks now, and I wish I could live in this bubble without having to answer any of the hard questions.

"Mmm, and you're not going anywhere." She kisses up and down my neck, purring into my ear.

Beneath her, my cock begins to harden, and I grind her down onto it. I'm insatiable when it comes to her, and we can never seem to get enough.

My phone rings, and she groans a complaint. I reach up to kiss her, to not let the call invade our foreplay, but it keeps ringing.

Sighing, I shift to glance at my cell where it rests on Taya's dresser. And the number that's calling is a New York City area code.

"Oh, shit." My heart starts hammering.

"What is it?" Taya's interest is peaked, but I think she's also annoyed I chose a phone call over foreplay.

"I think this is that radio station in New York. The one I interviewed with."

Her expression morphs into excited understanding. "Pick it up!"

"I'm going to take it in the bathroom, okay?" I point to the bathroom in Taya's room, the only one in the house that's attached to a room.

My hands are shaking as I shut the door and click to connect the call.

"Hello, this is Austin Van Hewitt," I say in my most professional voice.

"Austin, this is Peter from WQNH. We spoke last week when you had your interview."

Of course, I wouldn't forget him. I spoke to all the interviewers via a video call, because I couldn't get down to New York City for an in-person interview. I was nervous the entire time but tried my best to impress them while also remaining laid-back and personable.

"We were really interested in your experience and what you could possibly learn here at our station," he says, and I swallow hard.

I hold my breath, waiting for the high or the letdown. Please, please, let it be good news.

"So, with that said, we'd like to extend you an offer. It would be for the assistant producer position. You'd be working long hours, doing the work everyone else wants to avoid, and you'll probably hate us some days. But I started out in that position, and if you dedicate yourself, we have a lot to teach, and you'll work your way up."

Every cell in my body is singing with celebration. I don't think I've wanted to cry over much as a man over eighteen, but I can feel the emotion prick the back of my throat. This offer, this interview, is one of the only things in life I've actually gone out and *gotten* myself. No one but me did this, there was no nepotism, and I worked damn hard to *earn* this.

"Wow, Peter, thank you so much. I'm really excited about this."

In the background of his call, someone is singing. "Yeah, we are, too. Listen, take a day or two to think things over. If you want to accept the job, shoot me an email, and I'll hook you up with Human Resources. They'll go over all the offer details, salary, start date, and all that. But again, we were very impressed. I hope to be working with you soon."

There isn't much to think about. I mean, sure, there are a million things to think about. But in terms of if I want this job? Nah. I want it, all right. It's the one thing in this world I am completely sure about.

I thank him again and we hang up. My reflection is staring back at me in Taya's mirror, and I realize I'm full-on smiling. This moment is one I should always remember. I was just offered my first job, not to mention in the field of my dreams.

As I walk out of her bathroom, Taya is there waiting for me. She's on the middle of her bed, hugging her knees while butt naked, an expectant, hesitant expression on her face.

"So? What did they say?" She bounces a little in anticipation.

This is what I want. She's the one person I wanted to tell this news to, and the first person whose face I wanted to see after getting off that phone call, whether it was good or bad.

I sit down on the bed next to her, take a deep breath, and then say it. "I got the job."

"Austin!" Immediately, she's on me, hugging my neck and laughing.

We're celebrating together, and I realize I'm half in love with her. No, I'm pretty much all the way in love with her. We're naked, hugging like maniacs, and she's cheering me on after I landed my dream job out of college. With everything on my plate, I feel like my emotions are swinging like a pendulum. But this, right here, is the answer.

This is what I want. Her. This job. A future in a new city ... together.

"Imagine if you get the UN internship, too?" I beam at her, thinking about six glorious weeks in the city with her this summer.

"Shh." She places a finger over my lips to silence me.

Taya is extremely superstitious about the UN internship she applied for. So much so that we barely talk about it, and Bevan is the one who let it slip in the first place to me. She'll know in a few weeks, practically the day I graduate to leave this place, and all of our decisions seem to be rushing at us like a train that won't be stopped.

"Okay, fine." I move her hand. "But I'll just manifest that. Speaking of manifesting ... do you think you did that with your letter?"

I've been wondering that ever since Brian said it.

"Maybe." She tilts her head to the side, as if she's considering it. "How do you think that letter ended up getting to me, here of all places? And a few years early?"

I've pondered this, too. "You know, maybe it was fate."

"That's cheesy." She snorts.

"Yeah. But it's kind of true. We have no explanation of why it was delivered here, or why it was grouped into my grade's time capsule letters. And in the end, we got together because of it, or it led us here. Unless you want to call up Mr. Belding and ask why it happened."

She shakes her head. "Nah, I'd rather leave it a mystery."

"Where were we?" I climb back over her, feeling turned on and on top of the world after receiving that offer. "First one to make the other orgasm gets an *H*."

Taya looks at me, smirks, and then straddles my lap. "Oh, don't you know the only thing I do is win?"

Fuck, there is no way I'm ever going to let this girl go.

And just like that, I'm twenty.

It feels weird coming out of my teen years. Those were so turbulent, full of emotions and drama that seemed so heightened at the time. Settling into this new decade, I feel more relaxed and sure of myself in my own skin than I ever have before.

As of my twentieth birthday, I'm dating someone I really, really like and maybe even love. No, I do love Austin. Maybe I'll tell him that, since I'm no longer a scared teenager. Not that I didn't say it in that horribly embarrassing letter I wrote when I was a lovesick teenager ... the one that he *read*.

But I do feel better than I ever have at just being me. I have a great circle of people around me; I know exactly what I want to do with my life. I don't sweat the small stuff as much, and I try to let things slide off my back more than I ever have.

I had my interview with the intern coordinator at the United Nations two days ago. I was absolutely sweating as the translation specialist threw questions my way, switching from French to English and over to Italian. Though I was so nervous, I thought it went well, and he seemed pleased at my skill set by the end.

Now they're going to vet me, do some FBI background check shit, and I'll hear around graduation time.

Though I kind of wish they'd have handed it to me on the spot. It would have been a kick-ass birthday present.

Honestly, any kind of present would have been better than the *none* I received from my family. Talking about not letting things weigh on me, apparently, this wasn't one of them.

Because I'm feeling the rage build as I walk out of my last class of the day and still haven't heard one word from my family. I won't take this lying down; I'm not about to be Sam in *Sixteen Candles*. I may be laid-back, I may fade into the background, but for my own parents to forget my twentieth birthday?

No fucking way.

As I walk through campus, the sunlight streaming through the massive oak trees dotting the quad, my pulse notches higher with each ring of the call I just dialed.

"Oh, Taya, hi!" Mom sounds cheerful but distracted when she picks up.

"Hi." If my tone conveys my attitude, Mom is oblivious.

"How are you, sweetheart? Did you have a good day of classes?" she asks, chipper as ever.

With every passing second that she doesn't mention my birthday, my ire ratchets up to the next level.

"It was fine. Anything you might want to say?" I'm being totally childish, but it's my right to be at this point.

A pause. "Hm, I'm not sure. Was there something you want to talk about?"

There is a commotion in the background, and I can hear my sister whining over something.

"Listen, Taya, I have to go. We're packing for a flight. It was unexpected, but Kath got invited to—"

"So, per usual, I am an afterthought." My voice is so hard, it could cut the phone line.

Blood pulses in my eardrums, my fingertips tingle as that hot/cold, prickly sensation spreads over me. Tears dot my vision and that crushing devastation of being utterly let down pins my chest.

"Taya, what are you talking about?" Mom is incredulous, and I can tell she wants to rush me off the phone.

"It's my freaking birthday, Mom. You live forty-five minutes away. But instead of coming here to see me for the first time at college since I started my sophomore year, you're going to some bullshit for Kathleen that could be done on another day."

I start to sniffle and realize just how absolutely hurt I am. Just once, I want someone to pick me. I want to be thought of beforehand, have something special planned for me, or just be the first thing on someone's agenda. Is that asking too much? How many times is my heart going to have to break when my hope supersedes reality?

"Oh, *oh gosh*. Taya, I'm sorry. Shit, I didn't ... this meeting is important though, your sister—"

"Has taken up every inch of space and love since she got on that stupid horse!" I scream, not caring who hears me as I walk into the student parking lot. "That meeting is important? What, so my birthday is chump change? You know you missed it last year, too? And for my eighteenth one, I got a cake in a hotel lobby bar because Kathleen had a jumping competition in Toronto. Or how about the time you canceled my fifteenth birthday party a week before because Kath had some competition in Spain? You want to talk about important? I guess I'm not to you."

With that, I jab the "end call" button with my pointer finger and promptly begin to shake. Sobs shatter through my chest and thank God, I make it to my car and heave myself inside before dissolving into a full-blown breakdown.

It was always coming to this. Generally, I cry it out with

Bevan or Amelie, but this feels deeper. There is nothing that can make you feel more hurt than personal, emotional neglect when it comes to your family. It tears you apart on a soul level, and those cuts might scar over, but they never mend.

And especially when you take this kind of neglect over and over again, with the emotions being so pent up, there is no choice but for the fuse to blow after a while. With each interaction, with each time I'm left feeling like they couldn't care less about me, I get marginally angrier. Marginally more upset. Marginally more confused and hurt.

Until all of those little instances stack up and come crumbling down on my head.

Even though my friends and Austin were wonderful this morning, having me blow out a birthday cupcake and promising an even bigger celebration tonight, there is nothing that smooths over the fact that my parents forgot about my birthday.

That they have been forgetting me for years. Almost my entire lifetime.

That'll teach me to ever stand up for myself again. It's like the world has labeled me the person who isn't granted attention and slaps me down to reality when I try to reach for any.

Because even when I try, for just one moment, to speak up and put myself first, it doesn't work.

So much for this being a wonderful birthday where I feel more comfortable being me than ever before.

It looks like another year of playing second fiddle to everyone else around me.

29

There is something about Upstate New York when it begins to warm up.

The winters here are brutal and unforgiving, but once that passes, everything turns green and vibrant. The air starts to smell like summer, and it reminds college students of all the shenanigans we can get up to when the sun turns hot.

I take a drink of the beer I brought out onto the porch of our house, everyone else still out at classes. Talcott is barely visible on the hill above, the crest that watches over everything in this little town. The weather is finally mild enough to sit outside, and that's what I've been doing as I work on a paper that's due as a final grade in a few weeks. I can't believe graduation is rushing up at us, like water rising from somewhere you can't see. It could sweep me away, or I'll learn to swim.

Mostly, I've just been people watching. It's hard not to from out here, and since it's two p.m. on a Friday, most of the students who live on Prospect Street are out in their front yards, drinking and playing lawn games. Shouting matches start over Can Jam points, and the girls across the street are tanning with a sprinkler on as they sip out of champagne glasses.

At the house next door, I spot the mailman, and he's stuffing a package and some letters into their box at the bottom of the driveway. Lazily, I get up from the bench on our front porch and walk to the bottom of our driveway to meet him so he doesn't have to put the mail in our box.

"Hey, how are ya?" I ask jovially, raising a hand as he pulls up.

"Not too bad, considering this place is starting to thaw out." The mailman searches the box on the seat next to him and pulls out a bundle of envelopes. "Have a great day."

I take them and nod. "You too, thanks, man."

Rifling through the stack, I'm reminded of the last time I did this. When I found Taya's letter. It seems like ages ago, but the words my friend spoke last week still stick with me. Is she expecting more? Will she always? Do I even care about that?

I'm in love with her. That's what matters most.

Tonight is her birthday, and I told her I'm going to successfully get her into Stars Bar even though she only has a fake ID. I got her a birthday present, this book all about the Russian language, which I hope she'll love. But the thing I want to give her most tonight is me.

I'm going to take the plunge. Commit. Tell her I love her. I'm ready. Scared as hell about the future, but ready. I'd rather jump off the cliff than stay standing here and never know what could have been. Or worse, lose her.

With that on my mind, I almost pass over the envelope addressed to me. But then I catch the name of the company, the parent who owns WQNH, and my heart is in my throat.

My offer letter. The one I have to sign and scan back to them. The thing that will detail in writing that I have a job after I graduate—in my chosen field.

I tear it open, and my eyes feast on all of the boring details.

The starting salary is decent, just enough to live on in the city, but still too little not to be hungry and push myself for more. It'll be tight, my budget, but I'll make it work. I want this enough, and it's my ticket to the life I want to build. I'm going to be making money so that I don't have to move home or rely on my family. Other than that, the vacation and sick time is pretty standard. No bells and whistles because this is entry-level.

But I'm ready for the work. I'm ready to grind and make a name for myself.

I'm about to rush into the house, sign it, and email it to HR when a car pulls into the bottom of our driveway and blocks my car in. It's not one of my roommates, but I do recognize it.

And my stomach drops when the driver gets out of the vehicle.

"Dad?" I'm so confused; it's like I'm in an alternate reality.

My father has visited me a total sum of one time since I came to college. He was so disappointed that I chose the radio major that he refused to come see that dream in action. Well, that, and the fact that he's never been particularly interested in me as a person. My existence serves him; I'm the son he needed to produce an heir to the Van Hewitt line, for all intents and purposes. But loving me? Doting on me? Throwing a ball around or taking an interest in my dreams, imagination, or life? Nah, now why would he want to do that?

"Hello, Austin." Observing our surroundings, he frowns, deep lines crossing his forehead.

"What are you doing here?" My pulse has sped up, and I'm suddenly parched.

"You've been avoiding my calls, and your uncle needs a start date. There are things we need to put in order, Austin. Don't start disappointing us now."

As if he has ever accused me of being anything but a nuisance my entire life. I've never heard the man refer to me as anything other than a disappointment.

"It's been a little busy, what with me *graduating college* in just weeks." My retort is snide, and by the way his eyes flash, he does not like it.

"With a degree that will be useless once you move home. But enough about that." Dad waves his hand as if my passion is just a silly hobby. "I've come to work out a schedule with you and have you sign the lease on one of our rental apartments. Your mother is not keen on you moving back into the house."

Great, so they want me to go home to Webton, but I'm not actually invited to live with them. My parents are pieces of work. So I'm supposed to pay rent to my family, who owns the apartment building, and be thankful that my father is "giving" me a place to live. Fucking Christ.

His eyes rest on the letter, the one I was just so excited over and now want to desperately hide. "What's that?"

"It's ..." I consider, for a moment, lying about it. Passing it off as one of my roommate's mail or telling him it's a junk advertisement.

But courage like I've never experienced surges through my veins, and it's because this letter gives me freedom. It gives me an out from continuing to slave away as a Van Hewitt. It gives me an excuse to stop this ridiculous conversation and send him packing once and for all.

"It's the offer letter for my new job in New York City, at a radio station. And I'm going to be taking it."

If balls of fire could come out of someone's eyes, my father would have launched two at me right now.

"Like hell you are. Your uncle is expecting you on the strip mall project. You have a company to run, your family is counting on you." He's so angry, his voice is shaking.

"No, *you* are the one counting on me. Which you shouldn't have. You knew what I was coming to college to study, and I've never been remotely interested in the family business. There are plenty of cousins, male and female, who can take over if they want it. But it won't be me."

I'm shaking from the nerves, from finally standing up to the bully who has been plaguing me for eternity.

My dad is so furious that I'm afraid he might get physical. I take a step back, just in case he swings. At this moment, I wouldn't put it past him. And that right there, knowing that about your parent, is just sad.

"You will move home. You will take your rightful place in the company. You will be a figurehead of the community and fulfill everything we put you on this fucking earth to do."

Oh, shit. He really is whacked out of his mind. That, or he's never been told no before.

So I tell him again, "No. It's not what I want to do. I know you'll never respect that. I've come to terms with it. But I'm going to New York City. I'm going to work in radio."

His expression is lethal. "You are dead to this family. You hear me? You don't come back, you are dead."

That threat's like taking a bullet. My entire body is numb as he walks back to his car, slams the door after climbing in, and peels off down the street.

I am ninety-nine percent sure that might be the last time my father will ever speak to me. And although I finally defended myself and made the choices that would make me happy, it's crushing.

My soul is heavy, a weight sitting on me that I don't think will move or lessen any time soon.

And I have to pretend it all away tonight, for Taya's birthday. Because I got into a relationship, I allowed a person to pin their happiness on me even though it was the last thing I said I'd do. Everything I just considered moments before my father arrived, about telling her I love her, goes up in a puff of smoke.

I'm far too vulnerable, unsure, and dejected to confess my

feelings. What if I go off to New York City and she decides she doesn't want me either? I'll be utterly alone.

Something in me begins to crack; the pressure I've dealt with my entire life seems to have gone, but in its place comes a whole new set of expectations.

30

I t's a bold move, trying to sneak Taya into the bar in her bubble gum pink minidress she bought, especially for her birthday.

The dress draws so much attention that I think the bouncers, who are two kids I recognize from my freshman orientation, are about to swallow their tongues. I had to bite my fist when she walked down the stairs of our house, and it took all the effort I had not to drag her back upstairs and spend the whole night in my bed.

At one point, as they look at her ID and try to keep their eyes off her legs, I think they're not going to let her in. Her fake ID is not great, and with the girls all giggling from the shots they took before coming down here, they're a tad obvious.

But in the end, they let Taya in, and we high five when she walks into the bar. My hand is on her back, and with the sway of her hips, my cock hardens. I'm going to have blue balls so severe by the end of the night that I'll have to spend all of tomorrow in bed with this woman.

Stars Bar is pulsing, it's so electric, and Taya is jumping around on the dance floor and shouting to the music with

Bevan and Amelie. I'm happy she's having fun, and she seemed to love the book I got her as a present. It wasn't very glamorous, but technically we're not exclusive, and jewelry felt cliché. Her love of language inspires me, so I wanted to honor that.

Though I'm distracted as hell as the others party around me. I'm still thinking about my fight with my father earlier. And how I'll be floating through this life without a family anymore. The brutal brood I grew up with weren't much of a loving support in the first place, but the stark loneliness crawls into every nook of my body and begins to eat at me.

I know now that they will not be there for me. That my father might actually try to do something to make me suffer my choices. That thought plays in the back of my head.

Then there is the reality that I have to suck this up and seem happy for Taya's birthday because she expects to feel special because I'm the man she's been seeing—sleeping with—probably falling in love with. The pressure makes me rub my temples.

Taya grabs my hands and plants them on her hips, batting her eyelashes at me and licking her lips. She's on fire tonight, and I wish she could inject me with some of her energy.

Suddenly, we're flying almost halfway across the dance floor. Some girl pushes Taya, her beer flying out of her hand and spilling everywhere, and I steady her as the crowd undulates with the impact.

"What the fuck?" I turn around and say to the group of girls who just shoved her.

"Whoops!" The girl snidely remarks, looking Taya up and down.

I think I hear her giggle to her friends and say something about "underage bitches."

Taya seems to shrink and backs away. "It's fine."

I see the light go from her eyes, and all the sexy enthusiasm she was just sporting completely disappears.

"It's not okay!" I'm incredulous, yelling more at her than I am at the group of girls who shoved her.

Said girls barely pay attention to her anymore, and Taya is suddenly walking away from me.

My temper spikes, and I know I should just leave this be, but I'm pissed off and soaked in half of Taya's beer. I really stood up for myself with my father today, and she could barely muster a rude word to those assholes who put their hands on her.

I see her chocolate waves retreating toward the bar entrance as the strobe lights illuminate everything in red and purple light. So I follow, knowing that I shouldn't. No argumentative words exchanged after eleven p.m. are ever well received or end in a positive solution. I just can't help myself, though.

"You didn't say anything to that girl who pushed you."

These are the first words out of my mouth when I push my way into the night air, the Commons teaming with drunk college kids looking for pizza.

Taya stands in the middle of the brick pavilion, various restaurant signs lit up behind her, as she hugs her arms to herself.

"Would it have mattered? No one would have listened to me anyway. They're not paying attention." She grumbles this.

I'm a little taken aback by her complete shut down from the moment that girl pushed her. Sure, she's laid-back and doesn't love to confront people. But this? Something else is wrong.

"What the hell does that mean? No one listened because you didn't stand up for yourself! Do you ever just say how you feel?" I should not say this.

I shouldn't. But the anger that has been ricocheting in my chest all night since my father drove away has been bouncing around with nowhere to go. And this is its target, apparently.

"Are you okay?" she asks, her eyes shiny with emotion but still checking to see if I need a shoulder to lean on.

That question makes me even more ticked off, because she should be worrying about herself. Why the hell is she always worrying about other people first?

Whatever we're arguing about is not what we're actually arguing about. I've tried all night to keep my spirits up, but that fight is still clouding everything. I didn't want to ruin Taya's night by dumping my feelings on her, and here I am doing it anyway.

And Taya? She's completely shutting down when something that minor should barely be affecting her. Especially, on a night like this.

"I'm fucking fine. Jesus, have I not been having fun for your birthday?" I run my hands through my hair, trying to take deep breaths and calm down.

Not that it's working.

"You didn't have to come out for my birthday. I know we're not"—she points back and forth between us—"this is not ... well, you just shouldn't feel obligated. I know you're leaving in a few weeks, and—"

"This isn't about that. Damn, are we really back there? Downplaying my feelings? So you had a crush first, who cares? Are you always going to make this a thing?"

Like I said, fighting about something that we're not even mad over. But this argument is going to spiral until we decimate each other, I can feel it.

"Austin, I don't even know why you're mad right now!" Now she's getting mad, and it feeds my own fire.

"I'm mad because you won't ever truly just stick up for your-self. With me! With the girl in the bar! And now you're trying to make our feelings for each other some kind of pissing contest."

"You've never felt about me the way I feel about you." she accuses, her voice cracking.

She has no idea I was going to tell her I love her tonight.

"Taya, that's not fair. I didn't know how you felt, you never told me."

I'm trying to phrase this in a way that will defuse the situation, because clearly we're both too keyed up right now. Somewhere in my rational mind, I know that. And I don't know what she was originally upset about, but it doesn't feel like this is completely about us. I also want to stand up for myself, even though I'm aware you're just supposed to tell the woman she's right. But the entire time we've been together, this has been nagging at me, and I can't not voice it.

"You were aware of me. I wasn't aware of you. I don't mean that to come off harsh, or rude, but it's the truth. Maybe if you'd approached me, or spoken up, then we'd have met sooner or linked up sooner. But don't put that kind of pressure on me. Don't blame me for the feelings you had before we even had a meaningful conversation. I wasn't privy to that, so you can't fault me for taking a little time to catch up. To be invested in this at the same speed. It's irrational—"

Her hazel eyes flare; I swear I see flames in them, and I know I said the wrong word. I probably should have just agreed with her and shut my mouth. "That homecoming dance *was* approaching you! Sorry if I'm being irrational!"

Shit, that did not defuse anything.

Taya stalks off, teetering on her heels, and I chase after her. "No, you're not going to go home alone. It's your birthday."

I try to take hold of her elbow—gently—and she jabs it at me. Stepping back, I'm a little surprised at the dormant anger I seemed to have awakened inside her.

"Yeah, well, I don't feel much like partying right now. Hope that's not too irrational for you!" she screams at me and turns around to stomp off again.

I can see where she's heading—back to our house—the one where she certainly is not going to let me into her bedroom tonight.

Instead of continuing this fight, because it's getting nowhere, I just drop it. I make a promise to myself to shut my damn mouth and instead follow her.

I'm about two feet behind Taya the entire walk back to Six Prospect Street, and when she walks inside and up the stairs, I don't ask to go into her room.

What's more is, she doesn't ask me to stay.

P opcorn, salty and buttery, melts in my mouth as I swipe at my tears.

La Vita è Bella, or *Life is Beautiful,* plays on the screen in front of me, the theater empty except for me crying into my popcorn.

The old-time Cinema in the Commons plays foreign language films during the matinee times on weekends and thank God for that. Because last night was shit, and this is always the thing that cheers me up when I don't want to talk it out with friends.

There is something about dramatic movies shot on real film that just pulls at my heartstrings. The beauty of the simple acts of romance, a kiss on the hand here, a lingering glance there, that just does it for me. I always say I should have been born a lifetime ago, when the world was a simpler place, when men were gentleman and families actually stuck together.

At least, in my sulking, that's how I'm choosing to interpret this film.

Last night was a disaster, and drowning myself in salt, loneliness, and the Italian language feels right.

The door to the theater makes a noise as it opens and closes, but since I'm sitting up by the screen, I can't see who it is. Then Austin walks into the row, and my heart cringes.

I should have known he would come looking for me. I've been avoiding him since our fight last night and spent most of my birthday evening crying into my pillow.

"Bevan said this is where you come when you need to be alone." He's looking at me, but my gaze is still on the screen.

Ah, so that's how he found me. Bevan would not have told him that if she knew why I was upset, but I didn't feel much like talking to my best friends about this. I'd done enough talking, Austin and I screamed it out, and I'd done so earlier in the day to my mother. Bev and Am know that when I'm ready, I'll open up. I'm the one out of the three of us who internalizes many of my feelings and needs quiet, alone time to process just what I'm feeling.

Apparently, that time is over. "Guess that alone time is over."

My voice is cold and quiet. He's sitting two seats away, and that's probably wise on his part, because I cannot handle being so close to him.

Austin's dark eyes are genuine, and I know he's not going to give into my overdramatic attitude. Yes, I'm feeling sorry for myself. And I want someone to indulge me. He balances me out by being the levelheaded one in this situation.

"I don't want to fight with you. What I said, how I treated you, I'm so sorry. It was ... there is a lot of stuff going on with me, Taya. I shouldn't have taken it out on you."

So I wasn't the only one who wasn't fighting the fight we were actually having. And although I'm upset and semi-annoyed that he tracked me down, I'm never one to hold a grudge. Hell, I've been letting my sister and parents walk all over me for my entire life, and I always treat them nicely whenever they grace me with their attention.

And I just can't stay mad at him. I wasn't drunk, not by any stretch, but the words we yelled at each other last night were a blur. I wasn't even really mad at him, but at my entire birthday. He came to find me, and I won't make him grovel. We're equally at fault, and there was clearly something else going on with Austin that wasn't about me.

"It wasn't just you." I sigh, running a hand through my hair. "My family forgot my birthday."

"They what?" He blinks.

"No present. No calls. My mom couldn't even have her memory jogged when *I* actually called *her* yesterday. Claimed my sister had a busy schedule, a meeting of some sorts. I unleashed. Let everything I've been feeling just cascade out like some angry waterfall. I felt better after, to some extent. But I'm still so sad. I feel like they don't even care that I exist."

"Which is why you were in a bad mood going into the night." A lightbulb seems to go on behind Austin's eyes.

Now he gets up and moves to be directly next to me and doesn't hesitate to lace his fingers in mine. The touch instantly calms my rattled system, and I hate that last night was ruined. I'll forever think of my twentieth birthday marked by that fight, by how my parents forgot. It's not a memory I want, and I wish I could go all the way back and just ignore that my chosen family, my friends, really were there to celebrate me.

"I didn't want it to affect me. I should be used to this, I shouldn't be phased." I shake my head, the movie's romantic soundtrack sweeping around the theater.

Austin reaches over, puts my popcorn on the floor, and pulls me into a hug as best he can. The theater is old and the arm rests don't go up, a feature of polite dating-past. I bury my nose in the crook of his shoulder, inhaling his smell and wanting nothing more than for him to hold me until the lights go up.

"They are the ones to blame, not you. I wish I could scream

at them about how they're missing out on knowing an incredible person. Of course, it affects you. The things that our family say and do always affect us, no matter how much we're used to or expect that treatment."

He knows; he's speaking from experience.

"I just don't understand why they don't love me, why they don't care. I just ..."

My voice breaks, and I bite my lip to keep from sobbing. Taking deep, measured breaths, I blink back the tears as I nuzzle farther into Austin. These wounds cut deep, and I hate that I let myself retreat when those girls slammed into me at the bar.

But Austin's words didn't help. "Did you really mean it? That I always back down? Do you not like that I don't stand up for myself? That I'm ... irrational."

I push back from him, staring him in the eyes to gauge his reaction.

"Taya, fuck." He shakes his head. "I didn't mean any of that. I-I was in my own head, too. My dad came to the house yesterday—"

"He did?" This is news to me. "Why didn't you say anything?"

"I didn't want to ruin your birthday." He chuckles sardonically. "I ended up doing just that. It was before anyone got home. I told him I'm taking the job in New York City, that I'm not moving back to Webton. He basically threatened me and sped off. I'm pretty sure it's the last time I'll ever see him."

That statement makes my stomach drop like a stone, and the distant, lost look on Austin's face has me reaching out for him, pulling him into me. As much as I'm so angry and upset with my family right now, I can't imagine being threatened by them. I can't imagine them disowning me, or seeing them, knowing it would be the last time in my life.

"Austin, my God." I breathe, my heart breaking for the both of us.

"Nothing I said last night was about you. It was about me, about my own shortcomings and the things I feel angry about. I hate that I didn't notice you in high school. I hate that because of that, I've only just found you and I'm about to graduate and leave. I'm all fucked up about my move, my family, the things my father said. I wish I could take back every single part of last night and give you the birthday you deserved. I'm sorry, Taya. I ..."

He pulls back, so much emotion in his eyes, and my breath catches. Inside my chest, my heart is bouncing around, my skin breaking out in a cold sweat and goose bumps. This feels like *the* moment. The one I've been waiting for ever since I saw him in the hallway my freshman year of high school.

A beat passes. And then two.

"I wish our families were better. I wish they were more supportive. I wish I could erase all the ugly things I said. But just know, that wherever we end up in life, I will always be here for you. You can always talk to me, always count on me. I think you're the most special, unique person I've ever met. And I always want you in my life."

While his words are beautiful, they're not the ones I thought he would say.

They also sound suspiciously like foreshadowing. Like life will take us in different directions.

And while I appreciate him coming to the theater, talking this out, and making things right, I can't help the niggle of doubt in my heart that we're heading for the end of us before we even got the chance to be an us.

"So this is what it's like in here. I always wondered."

I turn in a slow circle, taking in all the equipment in the dark radio booth. Lights blink and beep, music posters from artists past coat every inch of the wall, and there are records stacked up in one corner. A giant Mac computer, like the hub or brain of the entire room, hums in the center of the desk, and pulled up is a library of what I'm sure are hundreds of thousands of songs.

"This is my mecca," Austin confirms as he nods.

It suits him. I saw his body relax the instant we walked in here. Austin carries a lot of weight and pressure on his shoulders, even now after choosing his own happiness over his family. Of course, I'm attracted to him in part because he's very confident and sure of what he wants. But there was something about him entering this space that highlighted that, that made me believe even further that this is what he's meant to do.

I sit down in a chair in the corner as he takes his seat at the computer and slips headphones over his ears. I watch him work for a while, announcing the song in that smooth radio voice of his. The one that makes my girly parts all tingly.

We decided that I should accompany him for one of his last shifts at the college station. He had to cover for a freshman and volunteered with ease for the graveyard shift tonight. I think he wanted to do one last one of these, even if it means staying in a school building until three a.m. It's nostalgia, and a place he'll never get to work again in a week or two.

There doesn't need to be any talking about how much this station has meant to him over his time here at Talcott. I can see it in his body language, in the way he flits around the room, rolling his chair from this control board to that one.

There are other things I've seen in his body language recently. Namely, that he's distancing himself from me. I can feel us slipping apart. Sure, we made up at the movie theater, but it hasn't been the same since. The way he's putting me at arm's length grows wider by the minute, and with finals and Austin's plans coming together about his move, we're spending less and less time together. For the first time since we became an us, I slept in my bed, alone, the other night. It was odd, and I hated every minute of it, but Austin claimed he needed rest for one of his finals the next day.

Really, he's pulling away.

What it comes down to at the end of the day is bad timing. We've always had it. I was too young for him to notice me in high school. I waited too long to make anything happen in college. If I really wanted to make my feelings known or follow that crush, there were ways I could have sought him out at a party or something and acted on it. But I waited until he moved into our house, without my prior knowledge. And then there was bad timing there, with the arrival of the letter. It sped up and forced us to confront things that would have come way later down the road in any relationship.

Now he's leaving. Our timing couldn't be worse. He graduates in a week and a half, and my heart is hanging on by a thread. I'm so happy for him that he's going to New York City to pursue his dream. That he's escaping Webton and all that comes with being born with his last name.

But I'm devastated for me. New York City is only about three hours from here, but that might as well be a lifetime. We're in such different places, and with all of our own emotional baggage, I know what the end result of us will be.

I haven't told him about the internship yet. That I'm going to be in New York for half the summer. Part of me knows that's wrong, that I shouldn't be withholding that information because of my needy heart. But the other part of me is holding out, to see if he brings up staying together on his own, simply because he can't live without me.

For once in my life, I want someone to choose me without me having to mention that I'm standing right in front of them.

"It's Frank Sinatra hour." He grins, looking back at me, one hand holding the big headphone to his ear.

Austin hits a bunch of buttons, adjusts some levels, and then pulls them off. We sit there as Frank croons on about a woman getting under his skin, and he gets up to come over to me.

He offers me one of those big hands, and I take it. Gently, Austin pulls me up and into his chest, and we sway as I press my cheek and ear to his chest. His heartbeat hammers in time to the music, and I want so badly to stay in this moment forever.

The enchanting track changes. Obviously, he already lined up the next song.

"What's this song?" I ask as the melody twinkles into the sound waves and through my bones.

"'With Every Breath I Take,'" he answers, his eye contact never wavering.

It's a romantic but heartbreaking ballad as I listen to the lyrics. About a man remembering a woman and the time they fell in love, but they're clearly not together anymore.

Slowly, Austin lowers his head and covers my lips with his. The kiss starts cautiously, every breath we take a gasp. It switches into something frantic but quiet. We're alone in here, and at the station, but this is still reckless and exciting in a forbidden way.

He lifts me up to sit on an empty part of the counter that houses all the switchboards, and my hands find their way under his shirt. Hands on skin, mouths bruising each other to the point of suffocation. We're trying, in this moment, to get out every last ounce of desire we feel for one another.

Austin taps my hip, a request to lift, and I do. He slides my leggings down my legs in one fluid motion, and I'm left in my Talcott sweatshirt and nothing else. He pushes his sweatpants past his hips and grabs a condom, sheathing himself before parting my legs and driving to the hilt.

I whimper, muffling myself in his shoulder, as all of our nerve endings connect. Austin's fingers find my chin, pulling it up to make me look at him. In his eyes, I see everything we haven't been saying to each other. We're connected in the most intimate way possible, yet my heart is so heavy that it might just sink me.

He begins to move, and we're clinging to each other while our gazes collide. This is love, what we're making. But it's also the end. I think we can both feel it.

I hold on to him, praying that I can grasp him tight enough so that he doesn't slip away and disappear after graduation. The sounds of Frank Sinatra drift in and out as he worships my body, and I feel the wetness on my cheeks.

I'm crying. It can't be helped, and if he ever asks, I'll chalk it up to the soul-ripping orgasm that rushes through me when Austin reaches between us to rub circles into my clit with his thumb.

At another point in time, having sex in the radio booth was

probably a bucket list item of his. It would have been a sexy dare between us. He would have bent me over and driven into me as he announced the next song to the airwaves. We would have laughed like naughty fools remembering it.

But alas, timing has never been in our favor. Because I'll look back on this, knowing it marked the death of us. And my heart will crumble to pieces every time.

33

AUSTIN

My phone pings with a message, and I delete it before even opening it.

I've been doing that a lot lately. You would, too, if dozens of family members were reaching out to tell you how much of a disappointment you are.

That's putting it nicely, using the word *disappointment*. Because the things I've been reading from my family members range from rude to downright horrible. One of my uncles told me I was a, and I quote, "fucking bastard little bitch who had a silver spoon shoved up his ass and was now shitting all over us."

So, that's what I'm dealing with these days. The Van Hewitt clan is in crisis mode, and they're taking all of their problems out on me. Not that they are real problems, or that they even realize that in the grand scheme of things, one person deciding to work in another city won't harm them in the slightest.

But it's a pride thing. A tradition thing. And my family is nothing if not traditionalist. If we were the royal family, I would have been fed to the press by now and ex-communicated.

In reality, my family has not lost a cent. They'll continue to rule Webton, to make money hand over fist, and move on in the way they always have. Soon, I and this scandal will be a footnote in their lives, and I'll only get the occasional bullying message or fucked-up outreach.

Though none of it will be from my mother or father. They've been radio, no pun intended, silent since he came here and found out what job I was planning to take. I fully expect never to hear from them again, and it's a heartbreaking sentence I know I'll have to come to terms with. Even if I hate them, they're still my parents. That kind of fracture in your life isn't one that's easily overcome.

The only thing I can do to stem the bleeding, to stop the ugly pain swamping my veins, is think about what I'm gaining.

My independence.

A career that I'm so passionate about, it almost makes everything better.

Moving to a city I've long dreamed of living in.

Working my ass off to prove myself and become one of the legends in radio, like guys I've looked up to my whole life.

But it's not just my family shit I'm dealing with. If it was just that, maybe I could get over it quickly. Maybe I could be okay with the fact that no one will be there to see me walk at graduation. My parents had the maliciousness to send one of my cousin's to do their bidding, to tell me that they would not attend.

If it were only that, I'd be sad but on the mend. It's this shit with Taya that makes everything so much harder to swallow.

When I took Taya into the radio booth the other night, I had no intention of having sex with her there. Sure, it's been a fantasy of mine, but I really wanted to show her where I thrive. What the environment I'm most passionate about is really like.

The sex just kind of happened. I put that song on, and the moment got to my head, and I couldn't stop.

I just didn't expect that the sex would be that heavy. Instead of feeling illicit, it felt like an ending. A swan song to this relationship we never could seem to hold on to from the beginning.

Every step of the way, it seems like I zig and Taya zags. I want to take a step forward, and something throws a wrench in our plans. We're two people so firmly in our heads, with our own doubts, that we haven't been able to take down those walls. No matter how hard we've tried, we're still holding back. It's not just my fault; it's not just hers.

She could beg me to stay with her. I could beg her to do the long-distance thing. But would that make either of us happy, at the end of the day? We can't seem to get on the same page, not for lack of trying, and it's breaking our hearts more. I see it in her eyes every day, and I know that inside I'm crumbling.

My world is in flux; nothing seems solid or steady at the moment. I don't want to leave her, and yet I know that if we can't make it work consistently while I'm at Talcott, we have no hope when I move three hours away.

She'll be busy with school, and I'll have virtually no time to dedicate to a relationship.

It's the mature thing to do, ending it.

So why does it feel like I'm walking away from the person I'm supposed to share my life with?

"You asshole!"

A door slams somewhere upstairs, and I shake my head, trying to bury it in my textbook and ignore the fight. I should be used to it by now, with those two, but Bevan and Callum getting into a knock-down, drag-out the week of finals is pretty much standard. With that much pressure, they're always bound to implode.

I wish they'd take their blowout elsewhere. Some of us are trying to study.

Or stop ourselves from having an emotional breakdown.

Since the night in the radio booth, Austin has been so distant. Graduation is just a week away, and we haven't talked about any of it. Not whether we're staying together, breaking up, giving this a shot. None of it.

I'm trying to ignore it, to just keep moving, because then the emotions can't touch me. None of this heartbreak can be real if I don't acknowledge it. Deep down, I'm aware of what a load of bullshit that is, but I can't take another person not choosing me.

I still haven't spoken to my family since my birthday, and I've been avoiding their calls. My mom sent a cookie basket, and Dad followed that up with tickets to a concert to see my favorite band in October. The gifts are nice, if not forced and late, and just an excuse to have me call them and make up.

Which I'm not falling for. I've bent too many times, have forgiven when it's my heart and feelings that are bruised. They need to make amends for this one, and a cookie basket is not going to do it. Our issues run too deep for that.

With everything going on inside my head and heart, the last thing I can do is deal with other people's issues. But apparently, the universe still doesn't give a shit about me, because Callum walks into the kitchen shaking his head, blowing breaths out of his mouth like he might shoot fire instead.

"Jesus Fucking Christ."

I look up, raise my eyebrow, and he rolls his eyes back at me.

Pushing the chair across from me out with my foot, I motion to it. "Sit down."

I'm done with this shit. Most friends wouldn't get involved, but I'm not most friends. I've also, recently, been accused of not speaking my mind. That ends here. I'm not just friends with Bevan. I've known Callum almost as long. And I'm not going to sit idly by any longer and watch this go down. She can hate me for this, blame me for their relationship being dead and over, but eventually, she'll be happier. I can't watch this go on any longer.

Callum sits, and I can tell he's on the verge of tears. For a guy so cocky, he regularly refers to himself as the "cat's meow," I know he's on the brink of devastation.

Maybe I can see their relationship with more clarity since I, myself, am actually in love in a real way for the first time. Maybe I can view it in the light I see it now because I'm about to lose the person I love, and there isn't a thing I can do to stop it. Maybe I'm just emotional and selfish.

It's probably a combination of all three. Taking a deep breath, I begin.

"Callum, you're like my brother. We've been through so much, and I know you inside and out. So right now, I'm not pulling any punches. We both know a lot of the issues in your relationship stem from Bevan. She won't get the help she needs, she won't even try to push through her trauma. But if you can't be there for her, if you can't weather this storm, then let her go. You're killing each other. This isn't healthy, and neither of you deserve it. If you love her, let her go. You are miserable, she's miserable. And I love her, she's my best friend. But I'd say the same to her, and I'd tell her that I told you this. Break up. Try to heal. Move on. No one can do this for much longer, it's toxic."

He blinks at me, then buries his head in his hands. I watch as his shoulders wrack with sobs, and I just want to lie down on the floor and weep from all the heartbreak in the room.

"I love her. I don't know how to stop doing that. And at the same time, I don't want to fucking love her. I hate it. I don't want to."

His voice breaks, and I see the tears leaking from his eyes.

My heart is already smashed to smithereens from what I'm going through with Austin, and now those smithereens just crush into dust. It's plain to see that he's so madly in love with her that the thought of losing her makes him want to lie down and die. It's written all over his face.

How can loving someone make you so horrifically sad that you hate them and yourself at the same time?

Would Austin and I end up like this if we stay together? Is this what love does? Destroys you until you don't even recognize yourself or the person your heart has always claimed?

It's only at this moment that I know we have to address the elephant in the room. We have to talk about whether we're staying together or breaking apart. Because this limbo is killing me, and if my heart will be broken anyway, I'd rather get the healing started now.

Just like I told Callum, if it is the end for Austin and me, I need to heal. I need to move on.

There is an atomic bomb-sized mushroom cloud of gloom shrouding the house.

Callum is currently on the second floor, packing up his room to move out. Taya and I may be unofficially avoiding each other, but I've overheard from conversations and pretty much everyone else that he broke up with Bevan. Apparently, this happens a lot, but him moving out is a fresh hell.

You can feel the sadness looming over every plank and board of this home, and even though I'm in love purgatory, I feel for them. They seemed like they were end game for each other, and now it feels like they're truly over. I can't imagine the kind of toll that takes on a person. I can barely eat and sleep with how upset I am that Taya and I are probably done, and we've only been seeing each other for a few months. Callum and Bevan have spent a damn near lifetime together compared to us.

A knock comes on the attic door, and I call for whoever it is to come in. I've been up here for hours, finalizing the last paper I will ever turn in as a college student. It seems surreal that this part of my life is just about over, and I'll be moving on to the real world. When you first enter college, you think of this chapter as being so far away. Suddenly, it's here, and I'm both excited and terrified.

At first, I'm expecting the guest to be Callum, possibly saying goodbye, but instead, Taya opens the door.

She ducks inside, shuffling her feet and looking nervous. It's been a couple days since we've truly talked to each other, and there is some unspoken agreement that we'd stop sleeping in each other's bed. It's as if we're dismantling our relationship piece by piece so it hurts less, but it still feels like someone is stabbing me in the heart every other second.

She's as beautiful as always, and I remember the first time I ever saw her in the house. The same shy smile parts her lips, as if there is a secret language she speaks that only I might know; we just haven't shared it yet. Her velvet smooth skin is on display in a white sweatshirt material romper, her arms bare, and the top of her breasts just peeking out of the top. Those long, luscious legs go on for miles, and I wish like hell I could just walk over to her and wrap them around my waist. All of her mocha curls are tied up in some white ribbon at the nape of her neck, and she looks both like the girl-next-door and some kind of porn fantasy come to life.

On the outside, she's relaxed and in home-mode. But anyone who knows her can read the anxiety and tension vibrating through her gorgeous body.

"Hey." She finally sighs, and just hearing her voice directed at me for the first time in days soothes me a bit.

"Hey. Come, sit." I pat the bed from where I sit in my desk chair.

Taya hesitates for a second, unsure, but then goes to rest on the very edge, as if she's scared to sit any farther onto my bed.

There is a beat, and she assesses me with those beautiful hazel eyes, then speaks. "I could come up here and make small talk. We could keep avoiding this. But with what's happening in the house today, I can't pretend anymore. I can't keep acting like this isn't going on. So ... what, um ... what is going to happen with us?"

Ah, so she's finally addressing it. I guess we're doing this, not skirting around it anymore. Part of me wanted Taya to be the one to bring this up, to show herself and me that if she wants something, she's going to get it.

I sound like an asshole saying that, but for someone who just told off his entire family to pursue what makes him happy, I need to see that she is also ready to live her life for herself. I only want her to be the best version of herself she can be, and I know she has so much untapped in there that is just waiting to be released.

"I don't know." I shake my head because I truly don't. "I've never felt for someone else the things I feel for you. You have to know that. But this move is going to consume me, this job is going to be all-hours, I'm going to push myself so hard ..."

"Do I always have to be the one to put myself out there?" She looks up at my ceiling, and I know she's talking to herself more than I am. "I know it won't be easy but ..."

Is that what she thinks? I could see how the letter makes her feel that way, but my God, I'm the one who went after her. Who had to win her back after I invaded her privacy, after I said dumb shit. In her head, I think Taya still thinks she's that freshman girl gawking at me instead of the confident, beautiful woman I've come to love.

Maybe that's my fault that she still thinks that. But it would only make this harder if I set the record straight. I need her to hold a little anger toward me, to know that she's better than what I could give her in these next two years. If that means cutting the chords to my own heart, suffocating my feelings, it's what I have to do.

"I never want you to settle for less. You deserve all of the attention and ... love." It feels strange to say that word to her when it's not connected to the other two I feel.

But if I give her those three big words, I'll want to keep her. Make her mine forever. If we admit we're in love, the pressure that puts on this, on staying together, on succeeding? We'll crash and burn so much more epically if it fails.

When she finally connects with my gaze, our eyes locking, I see anger simmering there.

"If I settle for less, because that's what you're saying I do in my life ... then you know what you do? You're so fucking scared, checking around every corner, following every rule that a Van Hewitt is supposed to, that you don't live your life for yourself. It took us weeks of back and forth and miscommunication after you opened that letter, that was private, to actually get our act together because you were so freaked out about being Webton royalty. And now you've finally stood up to them and suddenly you're the poster child for reaching for the stars? Don't shame me, Austin. I may have a fucked-up family, but at least I put my own needs and wants ahead of theirs, and I always have. Just because I'm not screaming and raging at them doesn't mean I'm not standing up for myself. I'm here, I'm thriving on my own, and I haven't forgiven them for what they've done. You act like I'm some doormat, when in truth I walk quietly and carry a big stick."

She's right, about all of it. My stomach and heart are in my throat, I feel nauseous and broken at the same time. She has every right to call me out, to rage at me. I've been distant and complicated for a while now. I just don't know how to see past it, especially in the state I'm in now with my family.

"You're absolutely right, you're not a doormat at all. You're the strongest, most inquisitive, special woman I've ever met."

"Just not one you think is worth keeping around," she counters, and I can practically feel the anger buzzing off of her.

"Of course, I want that, of course. It's just—"

"There is always a 'just' with you, isn't there? And this summer? When we're both in New York?" She's furious with me but still wants to make this work.

She's still willing to put herself on the line, and how the hell could I ever call her meek? How the hell could I think she doesn't stand up for herself?

She's a controlled burn, the kind of fire that knows exactly what it wants to accomplish and holds back until it can strike. Only this time, I'm one move ahead of her and won't let her extinguish herself.

Part of me wants to stop this right now. To punch myself in the fucking face and see what I'm doing to this woman. I already know how fucking dumb I am to let her go, but I can't hold her back. She deserves the most epic kind of love, and I'm not sure I can give that to her, knowing what pressures are about to be loaded onto my shoulders. I just got free of my family, it's selfish, but I don't know if I can take on a relationship while trying to keep myself afloat in New York with no safety net. It's not fair to her.

You know that saying? *If you love someone, set them free.* It's the hill I'm dying on right now.

"Taya, I just ..."

"You can't even say it, can you? You're going to make me do it? Coward. We should end this. It's done." Taya nods, like she's trying to convince herself and then stands.

It's not when she firmly shuts my door without another word that I know I made a mistake. I knew that a week ago, when the distance started. I know I'll regret this for a long time. Maybe forever.

I love her. We're in love, though neither of us has said it. And we can't do a damn thing about it. There isn't a name to what's keeping us apart or some tangible reason. It just ... is. And some-times, that's the only way to explain things.

But if it means she gets to move on, to fall in love with someone who isn't as fucked up as I am and doesn't need to work through shit, then I can take it.

Even if my heart is a bloody, mangled mess.

36

TAYA

I sit in the quiet, wondering how we reached the end of sophomore year and where the time went.

This year felt like a million jam-packed into one. We've gone through so many changes, all of us together. And I personally have grown more than I ever have in a calendar year.

I've lost innocence when it comes to my family. I fell in love. I achieved a dream, one that will put me on the path to achieving the one I've always had; to work for the United Nations.

My future seems bright, and at the same time, so lonely and gray. The living room is my most frequented spot now. Because even though it puts me in the direct line of fire when it comes to Austin walking around the house, at least I don't have to be in my bedroom. Where we've slept in my bed together, where he's explored my body, where we've sat night after night studying or watching TV. It's too painful to spend time alone in there now that we're not together. I have no idea what I'm going to do with this house once he doesn't live here anymore.

While I'm heartbroken and drowning my sorrows in every typical breakup ritual, I'm also angry—that he would pin this on me. That he'd make me be the one to actually come out and say we're through. For years I was silent, waiting for him to notice me, and when I finally spoke up and asked if he wanted to be with me, he didn't even have the balls to say a thing.

I sigh into the void, the house deadly quiet. No one is here except for me, and I should be upstairs packing to go home for the first part of the summer until my internship, but I just can't bring myself to. Leaving the house in itself signifies how over Austin and I really are.

Bevan and Amelie are at the library studying, Austin is somewhere that he clearly wouldn't share with me now, and Scott went to grab his personal belongings from his call center job at the student center.

Even though Callum no longer lives here, he went home earlier than the anticipated end date of the semester, Bevan has been avoiding the house, too. She's in a lot of pain, and I think being here just reminds her of him too much. I have no idea how they're both going to survive this, but it's necessary. That also doesn't mean something that needs to be done won't hurt like hell and feel like your world is ending, though.

The doorbell rings, and I rise from the living room couch to answer it. It's probably just a package or something. None of the roommates would ring the bell.

But when I get to the door, I'm shocked as hell to see who is standing there.

"Kathleen?" My forehead is full of wrinkles as I squint my eyes at my sister standing on the front porch.

"Hey, Taya." She does a small, awkward wave.

I look past her, swiveling my head, looking for—

"Mom isn't here. Neither is Dad. I drove myself."

"I didn't even realize you got your license." It comes out before I can think not to say it.

As I move aside and wave her in, Kath chuckles. "Somewhere in between my schedule, which rivals Beyonce's, I took the road test."

Mom and Dad typically just chauffeur her around, so I'm surprised she drove down here by herself. "What ... um, what're you doing here?"

"Good to see you, too." She smirks. "I know, I know, it's weird that I'm here. I've never come for a sisterly visit."

"And we're not close," I point out.

That might sound rude, but it's true.

"In that, you are correct. You look ..."

I think my sister is trying to give me a compliment but is clearly failing.

"Like I'm going through a breakup? I am." My laugh is so bitter it's not even funny.

"I'm sorry about that." Kath seems genuinely upset for me. "Austin Van Hewitt?"

My mouth falls open. "How did you know that?"

She taps the side of her temple. "We saw you at the mall, remember?"

That seems like eons ago when we took that trip to Webton together. "Oh, of course. I forgot. Jeez, didn't think you knew who the Van Hewitts are."

"I live in barns, typically, not under a rock. Of course I know the royalty of Webton." My sister wears a *duh* expression on her face.

Where I'm dark features and a rounded heart face, Kath is all sharp angles and fair skin. It makes her look far more intimidating at an equestrian competition; I've seen it.

"I came to apologize, and also give you this. It's from Mom."

She hands me an envelope, and I hold it delicately, like it might burn me. Ugh, another letter. Only drama and heartbreak have come from things that come in envelopes addressed to me.

"Thanks?" I hold up the letter.

I'm not going to open it here, in front of her. I don't even know how long it will take me to actually make myself read it. I'm dealing with enough despair right now.

"I should have called on your birthday. It was awful of me, and of our parents. I'm so sorry, I overheard your conversation with Mom, and ..."

She trails off, her eyes begging me to understand. "Sometimes I go off into my own world, Taya. And that's selfish of me. I should be a better sibling, do better. Sometimes I see you and Amelie and Bevan and wish the two of us had that kind of bond. It's always felt a little like you didn't need me, but I see how you view it from your side. What you said on that phone call, I hated our family at that moment. We were so wrong, what we forgot for you was so wrong."

Now I have to cry, because I've been keeping that hurt at bay. My breakup has taken front and center, but the sheer magnitude of what that birthday and how they forgot did to me all comes pouring down on me like an avalanche.

I'm swiping at tears, and then I feel Kath hug me, and my shoulder is wet from her tears. It's the realest moment we've had in years, in maybe our entire relationship.

We both catch ourselves and take a step back, laughing through snot and hiccups. Then we go silent, realizing the breakthrough we just had.

"I should go. I think that's enough for today." She nods.

"But you just got here. Let me make you ..." We have no food in the house, what with everyone leaving in a few days. "Uh ... I have alcohol."

"I'm sober, remember?" She made the pledge during a campaign for some sponsorship. "Sometimes my job really sucks."

It's the first time I've ever heard her refer to her sport as a job. Something must be happening behind the scenes, but it's too much to get into now.

"Mom is really proud of you, you know." My sister glances back at me as she heads for the door. "All she does when we're traveling is moon over how many languages you can speak, and how you're going to work for the United Nations doing such good someday."

"Really?" That's a shock to me.

"She talks about you constantly. How independent and smart you are. What a gem you are to the world. When she talks to me, it's just horses, horses, horses. Just once, I want to be a normal girl. To go to college and have her dote on me and wonder what good I'll do in the world."

"And just once, I'd like to have her undivided time." I shrug, my smile a sad one.

In another life, maybe we would have reached this conclusion sooner. Maybe we would have banded together instead of taking the roles of frenemies. Perhaps it's not too late to realize that we're not all that different from each other.

"We always want the other side of what we don't have." My sister gives me a sad smile.

"That's very true." In so many situations.

I'm about to bid her goodbye and shut the door when she turns around.

"When you come home, maybe we can grab lunch. Go to the mall for something other than riding clothes. Go to a party. I don't know, something normal?"

My sister shrugs as if she's embarrassed for asking, and I see her at this moment. Truly see her. She's just like me. Just trying to fit in while also going after her dreams. She wants things that seem out of reach, and is ... envious of me? I never thought that would be the case in my entire life.

"Sure. That sounds nice, Kath."

When I smile at her, it's genuine. For such a long time, we've been on separate pages. No, we've been in totally separate books.

This isn't a resolution, it isn't some happy-go-lucky family reunion, but we've taken a step in the right direction.

Through the fog of my shattered heart, I can see little beams of light peeking through.

I don't know why I have to be here for this.

There is an end-of-year house meeting among the roommates, and I had to give Scott my last portion of the sublet rent, so here I am. This meeting is really about those living here next year and how they're going to lock it up for the summer.

I should probably just leave, but I haven't been in Taya's presence for days, and I'm a fucking masochist along with a prick. She shouldn't have to see my face, but I miss her like crazy. If this is the last time we're in the same room, I have to stay.

"All right, guys, we have to talk about who is taking the TV home, who will be locking up last. I volunteered to come up here over the summer and check in on the place."

Amelie, the peacemaker, starts the conversation off, and I tune out.

I know I'm the one who let Taya go, who made her break up with me. Call me coward, asshole, fuckboy, whatever name in the book. I am all of those things. But I'm also in love with her and don't want to do what I did to her, unknowingly, for years.

Make her feel like less of a priority, like she always comes second. I've heard how long distance goes, especially between young people. I don't want that for her.

The girls are in the middle of talking about how to disconnect the washing machine—which is the dumbest conversation ever—when Callum walks in.

The tension and grief between him and Bevan is palpable. I know he left for Webton a few days ago, but someone clearly told him he needed to be here. And Amelie doesn't skirt around the bullshit as soon as he sits down.

"We need to talk about the house now that ..." Amelie trails off, at a loss for words. "Well, now that Callum has moved out and Austin is leaving."

My eyes can't help but land on Taya when Amelie says I'm leaving, and with the way she's biting her lip, she looks like she's trying not to cry.

I want to talk to her so badly. But what else can we say? There is no one reason why we're falling apart, why it's already done. Maybe for as much as we have in common, we were always too different from the start.

"Can't we just give it the summer?" Bevan sounds meek, which is so unlike her that it freaks me out.

She's looking at Callum, and I know this has nothing to do with the house. Sure, one could interpret that she's asking the group to wait it out, to see if they can all come back into the house junior year and live together like they always have except for me, whose room will be taken back over by Gannon.

But in reality, she's asking Callum himself. To give their relationship space, maybe for the summer, but not to give up on it.

"Yeah. We'll shelf it for now," Amelie interrupts, knowing that we all do not need to be here for this.

Taya is refusing to even look at me, and I'm growing more irrationally annoyed by the second. I know I'm the one responsible for this, but it was a freaking mistake. Part of me wants to take it all back right now, get on my hands and knees and beg.

We've been back and forth so many times, and I never want us to end up like Bevan and Callum.

Before I can even form a coherent thought about what I could do to get her to talk to me, I'm interrupted.

"HEYO!"

Gannon comes walking up the lawn, and I do a double take. The guy and I have never been close, but I know of him having grown up in the same town. I've lived in his room for about five months, and he told no one he was showing up here today. Amelie has her back to him, and she's smiling down into her phone. When Taya and I were on speaking terms, she let slip that Amelie finally found a guy who piques her interest. Well, maybe that's about to go up in smoke.

"No fucking way," Bevan deadpans and rolls her eyes.

Bevan is clearly so over the apple of Amelie's eye. And I can't say I blame her. From the stories Taya has told me, it's been a bad situation.

"What's up, party people?" Gannon opens his impressively cut arms wide as he throws the door open, that signature movie star smile beaming at us.

I swear, I think I just saw Amelie's stomach drop through the floorboards of the living room. As if in slow motion, she turns, her expression one of horror.

"Ams! I missed you." He marches up the steps, towering over her, and scoops her up into a hug.

"Oh shit," Callum coughs into his fist, watching the train wreck we all can't take our eyes off of.

Unlike the rest of our roommates, Gannon has no idea what's going on. First of all, the guy is clearly completely oblivious when it comes to Amelie's feelings. Not only does he not realize she's in love with him, but I've heard, from Taya, that he hooks up with other girls right in front of her. I've only lived here a couple of months, and even I know how mad about him she is.

So, of course, he's not going to think what he did on the reality TV dating show is a big deal at all. But there are five other people sitting on the porch, fully aware of how hurt and pissed off Amelie has been the whole time he's been gone.

"Get. The. Fuck. Off. Of. Me," Amelie grits out between her teeth.

And then ...

She punches him in the stomach.

Gannon barely even flinches, since Amelie is one hundred pounds soaking wet, but his face falls so hard that I think the guy is about to hit the pavement.

"What the fuck?" He wonders as she runs up the stairs, covering her mouth.

We all sit here, stunned by what happened but very much aware of all he's missed. I don't envy the guy for coming back now.

This semester, the couple of months it's been, has felt like an eternity. One I haven't wanted to end. But now that the party's over and the lights have come up, there is nothing left here.

I'm standing in a group of strangers; I'm no longer a part of this family I thought I was being adopted into.

A person knows when it's their time to leave, to exit stage left. And my cue just came.

38

The afternoon of graduation, I can't stop swiping tears away.

This morning, I heard the front door close as Austin left in his cap and gown. He probably walked across that stage with no one in the audience. Though I'm irate and miserable when it comes to him, that just does something to my heart. No one should go through one of the happiest moments of their life, something they worked so hard for, alone.

It's been extremely awkward in the house, and not just because everyone knows Austin and I broke up. Things with Callum and Bevan are depressing and strange, as is the fact that Gannon showed up. Amelie has been sullen and angry since he took off after she punched him.

We're all in our own heartbreak comas, trying to support each other, and huddled on the couch under blankets even though school is over and it's almost eighty outside. I think each of us has tears streaking our faces, and we should be packing but can't manage to pull ourselves from our grief. I also can't stop thinking about Austin and how lonely he must feel at graduation.

As if the universe conjured him, the front door opens, and in walks the guy whose name is still tattooed all over my heart.

He walks past the living room in his gown, his cap in his hand, and gazes at me. He opens that mouth, the one I miss so much, and looks like he's about to say something. And then he closes it and walks up the stairs.

My head whips to Amelie, who just shrugs, and I can feel the fury going from a simmer to a boil in my veins. So now he can't even talk to me? I'm doing that thing, the thing where girls spiral. But the dejection is taken to a whole other level, and we're leaving in two days, and I just ...

What the hell are we doing? Him and me? We can't make this work ... why exactly? And he never even gave me a reason. He never fought for me.

I'm so sick of people not fighting for me.

Throwing off the blankets and straightening my Talcott T-shirt, I march up the stairs on a mission.

When I reach the attic, I don't even bother knocking and throw open the door. Austin's head turns in surprise as he stands in the middle of the room shirtless with just the khaki shorts he must have been wearing under his graduation attire. On his bed are two large, half-filled suitcases, and those only serve to add fuel to my fire.

Pointing at the suitcases, I go off.

"Isn't that just fucking great? You berate me about not committing, about being scared to go for anything I want. When all I've wanted was you, and I thought this whole time it was me putting myself out there. It's so typical that you look right past me, Austin. That you'd leave me behind, just like that."

His face transforms from resigned defeat to anger to confusion and back to sadness all in the same second. I snap my fingers to emphasize my point, getting right up in his face.

"I'm so fucking tired. So fucking tired of being overlooked.

Just because I don't make a fuss about myself or the things I want doesn't mean I don't want to be special too. I want to be admired by the few people I let close enough. I want to be cared for like I'm fragile and incredible and no one wants me to break. Do you know how often I feel like no one notices anything I do? Every single day. I shouldn't have to shout from the rooftops to be given the respect and love I desire. But apparently, unless I do that, I'm not worth it to you."

I didn't fight for myself; I didn't truly speak my mind during the conversation that ended us. But I have nothing to lose now. He'll be gone in forty-eight hours. And if I have to live with these words trapped inside my chest for the next however many years, they'll poison me. They needed to be released.

"*I can't do this*." He sighs, looking down at the ground.

"You can't do this?" I harrumph, high on my anger. "Well, well, what a fucking surpr—"

"I love you!" He blows up, throwing his hands over his head. "Isn't that just the worst part of this? Of course, I love you, Taya. You think it would be so damn difficult to leave if I didn't? I'm sitting here depressed as hell instead of relishing every second of my future. I'm moving to New York to pursue my dream, and all I can think about is how much I'm going to fucking miss you. I'm trying, trying so hard, to put you first. You don't deserve someone who is over a hundred miles away, who won't be reachable when you need them. You deserve someone who sees you from the very moment they meet you. I'm an idiot! I didn't see you until it was too late, and now ..."

Fists dive into his sandy blond hair, and he looks like he might rip it all out.

"You love me?" I blink, all the air gone from my lungs.

Austin stalks toward me, his gorgeous face trained in a deadly serious expression.

"I'm in love with you. Every cell in my body is for you. I hate that I haven't said it, that I've been too scared to. You're right, about everything. I should have been shouting it, fucking screaming it. You're worth everything, Taya. Which is why I wanted you to have everything you deserve."

"I deserve you. I want you!" I cry. "I love *you*."

He's on me before I can take another breath, and we fall to the mattress.

"I'm never letting you go. Fuck the distance." He growls as we claw at each other.

Our clothes come off so fast that I can barely breathe in time with our movements.

"You better not. I love you. I love you," I repeat as he reaches for the nightstand.

In an instant, he's inside me, and this make up is the most intense, passionate experience I've ever had in my life.

Austin's eyes never leave mine, and I know for certain that we're not over. We'll never be over.

We may have a million things to figure out, but he promised not to let me go.

For the first time, I allow my fear to melt away. I'm putting my trust in him and giving into every ounce of love I feel.

We've earned the right to figure out our happily ever after.

My pillow smells like her again, and I wish I could bottle this moment up and carry it around with me forever.

"I wish we never had to leave this bed," I whisper.

"Me either," Taya whispers back.

Outside, a bird chirps, and the sun shines through my windows. My fellow graduates are probably out with their families right now, having celebratory dinners or being congratulated for this major life moment. A smidge of sadness creeps in, because I had no one there to cheer me on, but this is exactly where I want to be.

The only person I want to share this milestone with is Taya, and it's even better that we're naked in bed.

Oh, and that we're in love. Obviously, I knew it before, but to hear her say those words? That's the only graduation present I need.

"I hate that we're leaving tomorrow." She pouts, and I run my fingers over her silky hair.

"It fucking sucks. But it doesn't matter. Because I'm not

leaving you, I mean it. I'm never letting you go." I repeat what I told her earlier.

"You have no idea how much I've wanted to hear that."

"I'm sorry it took me so long to stop being an idiot. I was just ... I have had so much going on this last semester. I want you to be with someone who could give you all of their undivided love. I wasn't sure I was worthy of the job."

Taya shakes her head and smiles. "Austin, just because you have baggage doesn't mean I don't want you. I want to carry it with you. Haven't you learned by now, that we're so similar in the way we lay down our problems and pick up other people's? I love you for that."

"And I love you. Every part of you. I will hold you and care for you like you're the most fragile, precious glass." I'm quoting her back to herself, but I mean it.

"Well, you don't have to be too gentle." Taya reaches beneath the covers and puts her palm over my cock.

I just pulled out of her mere minutes ago, and yet I'm ready when she says go. I groan, tightening the hold I have around her and protesting up to the ceiling.

"I don't want to leave. I've never wanted to stay at Talcott more. Hell, I'd even go back to Webton for you." I'm not lying when I say that.

"I would never make you do that." She says this seriously.

Taya knows I'll rarely venture back there. There is nothing for me now. I'd do it for her, but I love that she knows how big of an ask that would be.

Kissing her forehead, I relish the moment. "How do we slow time down?"

"Well, we do have one thing to look forward to." Taya smirks.

"Another round?" I roll on top of her, my cock thickening as it hits the smooth skin of her inner thigh.

She pushes at my chest and laughs. "*No*. Well, yes. But I was talking about my internship. We'll be apart for a little, but then we have six weeks in New York."

Joy, pure and bright, seizes my chest. "How the hell did I forget that? I was lying here, gloom starting to take over at the thought that I don't know the next time I'll see you. But I do. And we have a whole summer to spend together in the most adventurous city in the world."

The thought of everything we could do in the Big Apple together ignites a new kind of excitement in me. And there's no doubt I'm asking her to come live in my apartment. It might be a shoebox that we can barely fit both of our clothes into, but I'm not hearing of any other arrangement.

"Now about that other round …" She swings up and straddles me, her slick wetness coating me.

This woman is attempting to drive me wild. Together, apart, or a three-hour drive away, we'll make it work. We'll make the most of the time we have together.

Until she's by my side, permanently. Taya may have spent years trying to get my attention, but I'm going to spend years proving to her just how much I love her.

Starting right now.

B eing home in Webton feels strange now.

I left the house and kissed Austin "goodbye for now" only four days ago, and my hometown has never felt so empty. Which is weird because it's not like we were ever a couple in this place. But the last time I was here, I was with him.

I've also spent so many nights in this house, in my childhood room, dreaming of the day he'd notice me. And now he's my boyfriend. Now we're in love. That fact makes me randomly giggle throughout the day when I think about it. For so long, I crushed on this guy I barely even knew, and now I've seen him naked, and he knows the spot on my neck that sends tingles shooting down my spine. It's a weird twist of fate.

One that I'm so freaking thankful for. He moved into his apartment pretty much the day we left Talcott. Drove down to the city and busted his ass walking all of his stuff up five flights of stairs. The FaceTime call we had when he was done and lying on a mattress on his floor was both sad but hopeful. I'll be there soon, and with every day, even though we're apart, I grow more sure that we're a forever type of deal.

I'm home for three weeks before I head to New York City for

my UN internship, and this period in Webton is sort of a test. My parents and sister have taken a big chunk of time off her training schedule to try to patch up the hurt in our family. After reading my mom's letter, which Kath delivered to me at college, my heart began to soften. I know we all have a lot of making up to do.

At first, I begged them not to. Kath has so much work to do before the Olympics next summer, and I've never said I wasn't extremely proud of her. I'm going to be there cheering her on like no one else.

They waved me off when I said they shouldn't take time off, and I'm more than happy they did. I know how difficult taking time off is for them, but they put me first for the first time in a while.

Since I got home, we've had family dinner each night, took a trip to the movies, and Kath and I have started watching *Gossip Girl*. She's never seen it, while I've binged it several times, and it's hilarious watching her reactions to all of the twists and turns.

Things are more easily patched between my sister and me, and I'm finding that the more time that we spend with each other, she's actually very funny. She has a sharp wit about her that I truly appreciate, and I'm both sad it took us this long to figure it out and happy that we're getting somewhere.

It's harder with my mom and dad. There is so much blame on my end and guilt on theirs that conversations have been difficult. I can see they're really trying, which is great, but it's just going to take time to heal.

"You have a letter." Mom hands me the envelope as she passes the couch and smiles warmly.

My stomach drops as I take it from her. Will I ever get used to having letters handed to me ever again? And why is the universe taunting me? She can be a cruel bitch sometimes.

Except when I turn it over, the handwriting on the front is

penmanship I recognize. And the stamp and return address are marked as coming from New York City.

Carefully, I slice open the envelope with my finger and pull out a singular piece of paper.

My beautiful Taya, the opening reads, and my eyes instantly well up with tears. He wrote me a letter.

Austin, the man I've loved for so many years, the one I wrote about, has written me a love letter. With my heart beating out of my chest, I read on.

This letter is far overdue, so forgive me. Also, forgive me that this is so sloppy. I remember reading your curly script in the time capsule letter and falling half in love with you just by the swirl of your writing.

I'm sitting here, on the tiny balcony, which is technically just a fire escape, listening to the sounds of the city. And I miss you. I miss you so much that my heart aches. That organ beats for you and only you.

The only thing that seems to make it better is the knowledge that you'll be here soon. That we'll drink coffees as we walk hand in hand through Central Park. That I'll school you in HORSE if we can find an outdoor court nearby. That I'll walk you to work, and we'll ride the subway together, huddled in a corner like all of those lovers you see in movies.

This summer is going to be epic, I promise you that.

I love you, Taya. You are the sweetest woman I know. This will be my time capsule letter to you, because mark my words, when you're reading this in ten, twenty, fifty years, we will be together.

Always,

Austin

I put my hand over my heart and find it beating.

For him. Only ever for him.

EPILOGUE

TAYA

One Week Later

It wasn't a question that I would move in with Austin for my six-week program at the United Nations.

Living apart would have been dumb, since we'd have spent every night together. This just cut down on commute time, cost, and I didn't have to live with a random intern roommate. Plus, living with your boyfriend in New York City with no chaperones and no other roommates?

That's the fucking dream.

There is a grunt and a whine as he pushes open the creaky front door of the apartment and hefts one of my suitcases inside.

"You have more bags for six weeks of living here than I brought for my entire life moving forward," he complains as he drags it into the tiny bedroom behind me.

"You promised me a summer to remember, and that requires cute outfits." I pout and then skip over to kiss him.

I'm just so giddy. The energy and vibe of the city has infected my veins, and I have a feeling it won't leave for a long time. The minute my parents dropped me and my bags off on the curb outside Austin's apartment building, I knew I was meant to fit here.

Maybe not this apartment, but it'll do for now. When we're older, more successful, we'll have one of those places a young couple could be proud of. Not that I'm not proud of Austin now. He scored a deal on this place since someone is subletting it for a year. Go figure, he's king of the sublet. Living alone, or now with his girlfriend for six weeks, is an accomplishment when first moving to New York. Though the place is just a galley kitchen, small living room with a table and chairs smashed into the corner, and a bedroom barely able to comfortably fit a queen, it's private. And it's ours to play house in for the next couple of weeks.

And my boyfriend has accomplished so much in a month here. He's busting his ass at the radio station. Working overtime, jumping at any chance for extra projects. Signing up for call times no one wants or shuttling guests to and from their hotels. Some of the work is beneath him, but he realizes anything might give him a leg up or a shot at being noticed. And he was just last week. He was simply chatting in the lunch room about some hockey trade, and one of the main sportscasters wandered in and was listening to him. The guy thought Austin had great insight and asked if he'd want to brainstorm about an upcoming segment.

Needless to say, Austin is over the moon. I know that while I'm here, his work schedule isn't going to let up. Nor is he going to stop volunteering simply because his girlfriend is living with him. I am more than okay with that. The most important thing we are both doing here is establishing our careers. Not that our relationship comes second, but I love how dedicated he is to his passion, and he feels the same way about my career.

As we unpack, the sounds of Radiohead float through the

small space when Austin turned his phone on. He sings along, and I listen, smiling like a goofy idiot in love. Because I am.

My cell vibrates on the bed, and I pick it up to read the message.

"It's from Amelie. She almost ran into Gannon at Target and had to duck behind a display of water bottles to avoid him." I chuckle, even though it's not really funny.

"Is she ever just going to either tell him to fuck off, or actually fuck him?" Austin ponders as he unpacks my bag of shoes.

The guy looks thoroughly confused as he keeps pulling pairs out of the bag. The poor man, he just doesn't understand how my wardrobe is about to take over his apartment.

"I'd bet on the former, if I had to guess. Things are bound to blow up soon. Especially since we're all going to be living together again come August."

Things with the Prospect Street house are in total limbo. Of course, Scott, Amelie, Bevan, and I are solid in that we will be living there. Clearly, Gannon is coming back to school, but I'm not sure Amelie is going to allow him to live with us. That charmer with a TV personality is trying everything in his power to get her to talk to him, to find out why she's mad, but she's been avoiding him like the plague. They are both in Webton for the summer, and Am told me he was waiting outside of her house twice a week. At some point, she's going to have to come clean, and he's going to have to wise up.

Then there is Callum. He is definitely on the outs, there is no way he can live there. He and Bevan are done, officially. There is no giving it the summer. Because she saw him with another girl. In all the times they broke up, he never dared talk to, date, or worse, kiss a girl. Then Bev saw him at the mall laughing with some girl in the food court, and she lost it. She ended up burning half the gifts he'd given her over their time together, and I'd been the one to go over there before I left and hold her as she sobbed until she passed out. Every time I looked at her, it was like her soul was ripping in two. I have no idea how they'll overcome this.

But I can't worry about all that right now. That's for next semester, and this is summer. I have dates out in the city to look forward to, nights with Austin cuddled up listening to the sounds of people and sirens and the noise of *life*. I have six weeks of my dream job that will hopefully lead to so much more.

If you had told me six years ago, hell, two months ago, that I'd be in love and living in a New York City apartment with Austin Van Hewitt, I would have laughed in your face.

But here we are.

I'm more than certain that we'll make it. That in two years' time, I will graduate and move here so we can begin our next chapter together.

After all, you never forget your first love.

Apparently, I don't have to. I get to be in love with the first guy whose name I wrote next to *Mrs.* in my high school notebook.

Maybe someday, he'll even ask me to take that last name forever.

Thank you for reading! While you wait for Amelie and Bevan's books to be announced, read another one of my spicy college romances, Nerdy Little Secret!

ALSO BY CARRIE AARONS

Do you want your **FREE** Carrie Aarons eBook?

All you have to do is **sign up for my newsletter**, and you'll immediately receive your free book!

Then, check out all of my books, available in Kindle Unlimited!

Melt

When Stars Burn Out

Ghost in His Eyes

Kissed by Reality

The Prospect Street Series:

Then You Saw Me

The Callahan Family Series:

Warning Track

Stealing Home

Check Swing

Control Artist

Tagging Up

The Rogue Academy Series:

The Second Coming

The Lion Heart

The Mighty Anchor

The Nash Brothers Series:

Fleeting

Forgiven

Flutter

Falter

The Flipped Series:

Blind Landing

Grasping Air

ABOUT THE AUTHOR

Author of romance novels such as Fool Me Twice and Love at First Fight, Carrie Aarons writes books that are just as swoon-worthy as they are sarcastic. A former journalist, she prefers the love stories of her imagination, and the athleisure dress code, much better.

When she isn't writing, Carrie is busy binging reality TV, having a love/hate relationship with cardio, and trying not to burn dinner. She lives in the suburbs of New Jersey with her husband, two children and ninety-pound rescue pup.

Please join her readers group, Carrie's Charmers, to get the latest on new books, exclusive excerpts and fun giveaways.

You can also find Carrie at these places:
Website
Amazon
Facebook
Instagram
TikTok
Goodreads

Printed in Great Britain
by Amazon

79187559R00144